THROUGH THE *Eyes* OF A BROKEN *Heart*

JAI

THROUGH THE EYES OF A BROKEN HEART

Copyright © 2023 by Janice Clarke

Bennett books may be ordered through booksellers or by contacting:

Bennett Media and Marketing
1603 Capitol Ave., Suite 310 A233
Cheyenne, WY 82001
www.thebennettmediaandmarketing.com
Phone: 1-307-202-9292

ISBN
978-1-957114-87-3 (Hardcover)
978-1-957114-77-4 (Paperback)
978-1-957114-78-1 (eBook)

About the Author

Jai is a Jamaican poet who for the last 23 years worked as an educator and restaurant operations leader. She now lives in Kentucky with her extended family. She is the mother of a 7 year old boy who is the apple of her eye. Jai honed her writing skills by documenting her life experiences. After teaching herself how to write poetry, she decided to embark on a journey to help others find their light at the end of the tunnel. Jai also has a passion for helping others and through her newly formed nonprofit, Sylvia's Hope Estate Inc., she focuses on families, especially children who have been underserved or abandoned. Jai holds a degree in Psychology and Business from Keiser University, as well as a Master of Science degree in Human Resources and Organizational Development from the University of Louisville.

THROUGH THE *Eyes* OF A BROKEN *Heart*

"Come into the car." I paused for a second and think to myself – who could this be? I turned slowly to glance over my left shoulder at the man who uttered that sweet command, then my legs did something my heart didn't approve - continued walking. My first glance was one of surprise, but without words the stranger's stare sweet-talked me into a submissive stop. "Where have you been all my life" he said. I peeped through the corner of my eye and my head convinced me that he looked familiar and that he couldn't be an abductor. He reached over and opened the front passenger door of his 1989 grey Nissan Stanza. The tight fitted jeans on my full figured body adjust itself as I gracefully sat in the front passenger seat. "Let's go for a drink" he said and I heard my voice saying "yes."

It was a sunny Saturday August afternoon. I felt bored at home and decided to take a walk. At 20 years old, this was a normal part of my weekend routine. I methodically parted through my meticulously organized closet and picked out a skin fitted blue jeans, plaid shirt and a white tank top to wear underneath. I turned around in the mirror and glanced at a perfect full figured posture smiling back at me. A pair of gold round earrings perfectly accentuated my low cut hair. Confidence exuded like sweat from my pores. I hid my eyes from the sun's rays with my everyday shades which also doubled as a cover for my soul. I lived within walking distance of town, and at that time in my life, a car was luxury. The mode of transportation was walking for short distances. Two miles would only prove to strengthen and tone my already curvy figure.

As I stepped into his car, my mind started to question my decision but I couldn't stop myself. The sound of the door closing reminded me that my fate is sealed. An occasional glance brought more details to my mind, but those eyes… He introduced himself and I knew there was no turning back. The conversation was probing and interesting and I was ready to tell all. A false sense of security overshadowed me and I forgot to ask where we were headed. I sat comfortably in the seat and was already sensuously transported by his cologne. God he smelled so good… I thought.

The car slowed and as he parked. I checked out the destination. Hardware store? Clothing store? Ice cream store? Why here? My mind wondered. The building had a roof top bar with a view of the town on the third floor. I wondered what awaited me. He opened the car door and shadowed me as I followed his lead climbing the stairs. This cozy hideout nestled in the heart of town had an ambience that I wasn't expecting. The sun hid behind the clouds the moment we stepped into the bar or "lover's nest" and the corner table had become our oasis. He held my hands while he spoke, and I couldn't stop staring at him. The more he spoke the more appealing he became. A 6-footer with dark skin like my mother, perfectly broad shoulders, well-groomed black, shiny beard, and a clean shaved head; Cream colored Linen pants, matching shirt, and brown leather shoes to complete the look. The highlight of my evening was his husky, yet mildly inviting fragrance that impregnated the air. The ambiance increased in intensity as the sun crept behind it's night cover. Lights of every color came alive and the sky suddenly became even more beautiful. I spoke openly and honestly about my previous relationship. He told me that he "had" a relationship but it wasn't going anywhere because the woman was "selfish." My heart fluttered with nervous excitement. How could I be so lucky to find this diamond in the rough – or is it him who found me. Full speed ahead, I thought.

He mentioned that he had buried his father a few days prior, and I came along at an ideal time. He had a way with words. Everything sounded like music to my ears. The night had to be cut short. He worked in the second city and had to leave to prepare himself for his work week. As we made arrangements to see each other again, we exchanged phone numbers and he drove me home. The slow drive tripled the usual 5 minutes distance as he savored the moments with me. He opened the door and held my hand to assist me out of the car. He's a perfect gentleman, I thought. "Can I hug you" he asked and my "yes" came before my brain could process his question. Lost in his embrace, I held him as if my life depended on it. My mind wandered to the future... is he the one? I leaned further into the embrace because I didn't want it to end. He whispers in my ear "today is the first day of the rest of our life because I've found everything I need." My mind went into a spin as his gentle squeeze is released. He watched as I strutted down the short walkway to my burglary bared verandah. I opened the padlocked bars, then the door, went inside, and peeked through the curtain to watch him drive off into the night. The first goodbye felt good because I knew he would return soon. The prospects were high and a taste of blissful joy caressed me to sleep.

The minutes seemed like hours, perhaps days. I yearned for the sound of that deep sensuous voice. I kept the phone really close so I wouldn't miss a ring. I listened as my sisters chatted with each other in the adjoining room, but didn't care to join them. My heart was singing its own tune. Midnight came and went and the silence became deafening. The thunderous beats of my heart heightened by anxiety scared me, and for the first time I realized how trapped I was. Reluctantly, I turned off the lights, pulled the covers, and dropped into my plush oversize pillow. This pillow use to be my best friend. Tonight it felt like a foe. It used to comfort my loneliness and soothe me to sleep. Now it irritated me. I reminisced his embrace as my mind walked all over me. Did he get home safe? Is he thinking about me as much as I am thinking about him? The day's events played slowly in my mind like a broken record and before I knew it, sleep stole me away. The chime of the alarm pelted, and I panicked. I couldn't believe that it was already morning. 7am meant catering and organizing events. I managed a park/restaurant and at this time of the year, group bookings were up. Although I had a long hectic day, I couldn't help thinking about him. I wondered if he felt the same way about me as I do him. After all I shouldn't be so in love, I only met him a few hours ago. Is he going to call though?

The taxi pulls up to my gate and I hurriedly disembarked to check the answering machine. There were no messages. Disappointment heightened the fatigue and as I flung myself across the bed, kicked off the shoes and greeted my pillow with the worst attitude. By now, it was dark and I struggled to stay awake. As I drifted off, the muffled ringing sound of phone awakened me. Disappointment quickly turned to relief and nervous excitement and by the end of the first ring, I grabbed the phone. "Hi baby, how are you?" said the deep massaging voice on the other end of the line. "I'm ok" I responded through a nervous grin. "I'm better now that I hear your voice" he said. The butterflies awoke in my stomach, goose pimples popped out on my body and my heart's band commenced its orchestra. His voice did a number on me that I couldn't understand or control. I forgot how upset I was and agreed to meet him on Tuesday. His mother lived in the area a couple of miles from my house. The energy from the phone call gave me enough umph to take a shower and settle in for sweet dreams.

The alarm went off reminding me once more that duty calls. One more day before my heart beats again, I thought. I had recently completed my associate degree in hospitality and tourism management that May. I took this job to pass the summer since my dream was to work at a hotel on the north coast. I crawled lazily out of bed and went through my daily routine – shower, grab a bite and go. I counted the hours to get home for my phone call. He promised to call when I got home. 5pm couldn't come any sooner. Anxiety and excitement consumed me as I hustled to get home, but the inconvenience of public transportation brought me back to reality. I settled down on the love seat in the family room to dinner and a movie after a cold shower, but the phone accompanied my every move. As the minutes turned into hours, the events of the day began to wear me down and I drifted off into a light sleep. I turned the ringer on extra loud for fear of not hearing it. The sound of a tornado warning blared, and I sprinted off the chair. After a few seconds, I answered without looking at the caller ID. "May I speak to Tony Please" said the female on the other side of the line. "Sorry you have the wrong number" I replied. I glanced at the clock, slammed the phone down and went into my room. As I drew the covers, I prayed – Lord please let me hear his voice so I can have sweet dreams. My sisters noticed that something was different about me, but only spoke about it between themselves. The engines of the freight trucks roared as they descended the slope on the road near the house. Although I lived in a community on the outskirts of town, I could still hear the traffic in the still of the night……. or early morning as if the road was by my window. The housing development was one of the older developments in the area and my grandfather had purchased the house in which I lived with my two older sisters. It was a two-family house and my uncle occupied the other side. Each apartment had 3 bedrooms. My grandfather lived in a community deeply nestled in the rural area of the parish. So did my parents as well as my youngest sister. I was 13 years older than my youngest sister and the other 3 sisters were a year apart.

My watch on the night got overwhelming at 3 am and I began to dose off. The sound of ringing confused me and I reached over to turn off the alarm. Another ring made me realize that it was not the alarm, but the phone. Who could be calling at this time? I thought. I grabbed the receiver and pasted it to my ear. "Good morning baby" He said in a low, husky, sexy morning tone. My heart skipped a beat as I responded in what I thought was my bedroom voice that struggled t o hide my excitement. "Good morning sweetheart." The sound of that voice made everything okay and I soon forgot my grueling night. I hugged the receiver as if it were him in my bed. He apologized for the late call, but I didn't care because all my wrongs were right. The conversation was light with expressions of yearnings. The parting was now "see you later" as the alarm went off. 6 Am duty calls. I had an unusual pep in my step and time was on my side. Getting ready for work had never felt so good especially after a night where good rest wasn't on the menu.

Nothing could go wrong today, I thought to myself. Everything was so easy and everyone noticed my new pace and confidence. Public transportation issues didn't matter today. I patiently waited for the taxi and even the driver noticed that something had changed.

That evening, the shower was timely and thorough. The black skin fitted jeans and pink polyester low-cut blouse waited to be perfectly fitted on my 5'11" voluptuous figure. As I applied my special perfume, I reminisced on that first hug and anticipation filled my stomach. My sisters became aware of my "hot" date when they noticed my elegant attire as well as my glow. They knew that it was extra special because of my exuberance. I waited on the sofa and before long, the Nissan rolled in like a limousine. I went to open the gate for my knight as he alighted from the car. I attempted to calm my flattering heart but "those eyes" peered so deep into my soul that I couldn't help but giggle like a child with a new toy. His long sleeve white cotton shirt and dark colored pants must have felt lucky to be on that body. Afraid that he was going to hear the drumming that was going on inside of me, I asked him for a few minutes. I went to the bathroom to make sure that everything was in place and then informed my sisters that I was leaving.

His embrace engulfed me and it felt like home. I struggled to pull myself away from him – he smelled so good, he felt so good and I whispered to myself "he's the one." "You look beautiful" he said and I melted all over again. He opened the door and ushered me into his car. I wished time would stop so the moment would last forever. That was not to be as the clock on his dashboard displayed 9pm. He pulled me close and gently perused my lips with soft voluptuous kisses. I grasped for air as the "band" continued to play in my chest. My knees felt weak, my muscles relaxed to the point where I felt as if I was floating in midair. I knew I had to regain my composure since I thought it was too soon to be lost in love. So, I reached deep inside me and mustered up the courage to snap out of it. The 5 minutes' drive to the moonlit bar was like a ride to heaven. Dinner and conversation were enough for me because any time is always better than no time. He mentioned that he had to leave soon to take the ride home for work in the morning. I wanted to go home with him because I was aroused and helplessly attracted to him but my moral compass chipped in. I took the last sip and he helped me out of my chair and held me all the way to the car. The power of his embrace subdued me once more and a web is woven from which I could not escape. He appeared to be the strong one and remained in control. A facade of strength allowed me to let go. He got out and played the part of a perfect gentleman from beginning to end. I had never had such an experience. Chivalry was always something I admired and valued in a man and he didn't disappoint. He waited for me to go inside and lock the door before he went back to his car. I peeped through the window until the car disappeared into the night. Still captivated by him, I lay across my bed and relived the moments. My mind is now in a spin, but I managed to lock in that capsule of time that meant the world to me. Sleep knocked at my door and I answered with a broad smile.

Friday morning came and I was elated. He didn't work on the weekends so I looked forward to his visits. He made plans to pick me up after work that night so we could hang out at the weekly "Fishy Business" (an after-work party held at my workplace). I had invited him and he agreed to hang a little before taking me home. As I scanned the crowd for his breathtaking physique, my patience grew thin. It was approaching 9pm and the event is scheduled to end at 11pm. Just a glimpse would set everything in the right direction. I continued to mingle with the patrons, all the while peering in the venue and hoping those eyes would make my night. I slipped out of the crowd to clear my mind. A familiar voice greeted me -"Hi baby" - and anxiety turned into excitement. We fell into each other arms without question. He sat at the bar and watched me as I did my rounds. Whenever our eyes locked, my heart moved higher in my chest. I was shy, excited, nervous, and happy. It was 11:15pm so I closed off, did my checks and was ready to leave. We discussed the details of my job on the short ride home. He mentioned that he didn't like my job and encouraged me to back to college so I could make a better living. I welcomed the idea since I had always wanted to enlarge my scope. The 10 minutes ride home felt like 2 minutes when he told me that he had to go back home. My bubble broke and I suddenly realized that I had to make do with the short time I had with him. I asked no questions because I was somehow grateful for the small moments. The goodbyes started getting a little more difficult each time. This time it felt as if a piece of me died. My yearning for a night in his arms made me irritable, but his kisses always sooth those thoughts away.

As the cold tap water washed away the week, my mind replayed the miniscule moments and although I was not a "shower singer", found myself humming until LeAnn Rimes "feels like home" came forcefully in my mind as if I was at a live performance. My sisters enquired about my mood since they had never seen me so cheerful, especially on a Friday night. My chuckles were infectious even when the joke wasn't even funny. My response – "I met the man of my dreams."

My usual replay of my day took place, but this time it was about college. I attended Primary school in the rural community where I grew up. By the tender age of 10, I was successful in the Common Entrance examination and was placed at one of the best traditional high schools in the adjoining parish. While in primary school, I dreamt of becoming a highly successful hotel manager and set a goal to earn a PhD by 30 and lecture part time at one of the island's finest tertiary institutions. At 15 years old, I graduated high school and decided to get a job since my parents weren't able to afford me a college education. My eldest sister had graduated high school a year earlier and was enrolled in continuing education (pre-college). My middle sister introduced me to a government program (that she was a part of) that offered job experience and a stipend for young people wishing to enter the work world and I wasted no time applying. The month-long camp type training was geared towards introducing youth to work processes and helping them to choose viable careers. It would be my first time away from home for any extended period of time, but I was elated. I had a positive outlook on most things and a tendency to see the glass half full. My mother was not entirely thrilled with the idea, but was confident in my ability to rise to the occasion and handle myself with respect.

The "camp" as it was called was a whole new experience from anything I had ever gone through. We were transported to a facility in Oak Valley, which seemed like a whole other world away from where I lived. There were approximately 40 participants, and they were bursting through the seams with excitement for an opportunity to make good of their lives. As we approached what appeared to be a more developed area, I noticed a big sign "Oak Valley Show ground next right turn." I peered through the window and saw men dressed in army outfits. My curiosity heightened and my excitement was dampened. Was this an army camp? I thought. The bus came to a halt, and everyone got off. The soldiers came to greet us and demanded that we form a line up in an open area. A petite middle-aged lady introduced herself as the center manager and welcomed us to the facility. Mrs. Williams asked each soldier to introduce themself and as they did so, my confidence grew thinner. "What did I get myself into?" "Is this military training posing as a youth service program?" I kept quiet since I didn't want anyone to think of me as a wimp. After a short debrief, everyone was whisked off to where they would stay. Female and male participants were led separately to their respective areas. Each participant had to find a bed and place their "stuff" on it. A soldier with a giant stature barked commands "dinner will be served in the dining room at 1600 and everyone is expected to be early. You will be informed of the operating procedures of this camp." Fear set in and excitement became a distant emotion. Everyone seemed confused because their expectations were dashed. I was ready to go back home. While we waited for dinner time, one of the soldiers' demonstrated how to make the beds (half the size of the one she had at home). Bottom sheet with no wrinkle, top sheet neatly folded and wrapped across the bed, 12 inches from the top. Personal effect such as toothbrush, toothpaste, soap, comb and brush had to be neatly positioned on top of the flat sheet, in a straight line.

Day one brought many to tears because it was an extremely frightening experience – but for me, I coached myself into thinking of it as a learning experience. The first night was most challenging. This meant adjustments of every sort. I had 3 siblings with whom I lived, and sleeping in a dormitory with 25 females was a huge undertaking. I was the youngest and although my appearance was one of maturity, my experience, or lack thereof gave me away. The 6 shower stalls barely had any privacy and I knew this wasn't going to be an enjoyable trip. The clock ticked louder, snores among chatter gave me a headache and tears welded up in the corner of my eyes. "Lord help me to get through this" I prayed and hoped for the best. "Wake up, wake up, time to get up" barked a loud baritone voice. The sound of a whistles rang out in the still of the morning. I glanced at the clock out of one eye that was awake and saw that it was 5am. Puffing faces afraid to show their extreme disgust strolled into the bathrooms to prepare for PT (physical training). "Half hour everyone on the pavement for roll call. No one should be absent" blurted a tall shadow at the door. All were gathered in the quad directly in front of the dormitories in record breaking 10 minutes.

My athletic abilities had not been explored since I was a full figured young lady, and didn't think that this would have been a win for me. I briefly tried sports involving strength (shot put and discus) while I was in high school. Soldier Plumber explained the routine after roll call. "We will stretch to warm up, jog for half hour, and then finish off with cool down exercise! Any questions, speak now." He shouted in an almost angry tone. It was dark and we jogged along a paved path struggling to keep up. After 10 minutes of jogging, my legs begged to stop. Another soldier who was jogging in the back of the group shouted "come on work those lazy muscles." I surprised myself when I realized that I was back in the quad. Everything was systematic and organized. 45 minutes to breakfast meant hustling to shower, dress and spotlessly clean the one area that each participant is solely responsible for, "THE BED." One bathroom with 6 shower stalls. Complaints were numerous, and while most made every effort to comply with the requirements, others decided to push back. While at breakfast, the soldiers checked the dormitories to ensure that their orders were being followed. During breakfast, Mrs. Williams asked everyone to remain in the dining hall for a brief meeting with the soldiers. "We are the only leaders in this room." He said. "For the duration of the next 4 weeks, you will do exactly what you are told." The silence was deafening. "Beds that are not made to standard will be tossed through the window along with everything else. You are dismissed!" Stone cold and obdurate, he left the room.

It was already 8:30 am and sessions started at 9. Half hour to pick up the mattresses from outside, make the beds and organize the toiletries and shoes. A few of the participants used the time to pack their bags and headed towards the gate. The grounds were draped with 7 feet high chain-link fence with razor wire on top. Leaving wasn't an option as soldiers with guns drawn stood on guard. Group dynamics had to be worked out sooner than later as lessons were being taught at a fast pace. There was no time for leisureliness as consequences came without question. Military standards were high and felt unattainable at times. Failure for one meant failure for all, so the pressure was intense for the weaker ones. Conformation was inevitable since no one wanted to be punished for something they didn't do. Intimidated and humiliated, the small group returned to their dorm.

First class for the day proved to be very interesting. It took the form of a seminar on table etiquette and the lighter side of the soldiers came out. Lunch took on the same format as breakfast and dinner brought a more relaxed ambiance. During dinner, the elements of table etiquette were practiced and inspections were done to confirm learning. Inspections continued at every break, and beds were pushed out of the windows like a mother bird does her chicks. After dinner, the participants were promised an early bedtime and all celebrated.

2 am brought on a state of fear and submission by the hands of the soldiers. "What could I have done to deserve this?" I thought. As the sound of blaring whistles, fire alarms and loud voices propelled its way through the dormitory, panic and disbelief glued me to the bed.

"Leave the building, go to the quad" they shouted. I was skimpily clad in my "bed clothes" so I hurriedly attempted to change them. "Leave as you are" said a loud voice. I looked up to big eyes staring back at me. Nervous and intimidated, I followed the other girls to the quad where the boys were also assembled. A roll call was done and after everyone was accounted for, the lead soldier Plumber explained to us that the exercise was meant to teach us survival in the event of a fire or other emergency which involved evacuation. Sighs of relief were short lived when he mentioned that this would be a normal part of our routine for the remainder of the stay. He further explained that each one should care for everyone else and the stronger ones need to help the weaker ones to safety. Emotional and tired, I crawled back into bed. Anticipation of "fire drills" and "physical therapy" made sleep a distant goal. They repeated themselves in quick succession.

The thought of "Home" had never been so enticing. No contact from the "outside" was allowed. Cell phones were a luxury and it wouldn't even make sense to have one because we couldn't use it. 15 years old and away from home for the first time among strangers was a hard pill to swallow. But I was determined to win and make the best of the experience as well as save face. So, I participated in all the activities with an upbeat and high spirit. Before long, I was given leadership roles much to the despair of 2 of the girls, Cassandra and Kenisha. These girls were much older than me and thought that the leaders were playing favoritism. Being the strong headed person that I was, I overlooked everything that they said about me and displayed my abilities even more. They were furious. Mrs. Williams had a short meeting with the group and explained to them that there's room for everyone to be recognized if they worked hard to succeed. The first week came and went. New experiences overshadowed old ones.

"PT" and "fire drills" became less wrenching. Daily inspections were sparsely done. I became instrumental in teaching others how to succeed in their daily chores which meant less "punishment." Beds remained immaculate and I felt as if the humdrum routine was defeated. Mundane tasks made way for interesting ones. Daily classes saw a myriad of presenters on various aspects of work life and life skills. My motivation was high and my focus never faltered. "I could use these lessons when I get to manage my hotel" I thought to myself.

Week two came and went. We enjoyed learning the group songs to help us forget the rigors of "PT."

"Oh when I die

No bada bury mi at all.

Jus lay mi dung

In a di alcohol

One quart a white rum

From mi head to di grun

Jus lay mi dung in a di alcohol

Week 3 arrived and excruciating pain in my armpits woke me up in the wee hours of the morning. I used my mini-mirror to investigate. There were a number of huge carbuncles in and around the area. Unsure and afraid, I bore the pain and went back to bed. During PT one of the soldiers noticed that I wasn't my usual bubbly self and enquired of me. Within an hour I was whisked off to the nearby emergency room at the May Pen Hospital, since the pain had increased to unbearable levels. The doctor looked at my armpits and told me that I had eleven boils, possibly caused by an allergic reaction. Someone may have used my deodorant. He further explained that he would need to slit each of them in order to release the mucus that is in it (using a blade and a syringe). No anesthesia made my situation worst. The ordeal was unbearable, and although there were two nurses assisting the doctor, they could barely contain my kicking and screaming. Pain medication was administered orally and a penicillin injection. After lying down for an hour to "cool off," the center manager, Mrs. Williams brought me back to the camp site, where I was allowed to rest for the remainder of the day. An arm brace that made me look like a duck with outstretched wings became a part of my attire for the next couple of days. I had become a favorite of the camp staff and while I rested, they would take turns to visit me. I soldiered on through all the activities in spite of my "surgery."

Graduation day and awards ceremony brought bitter sweet moments. This meant it was time to go home, end of torture and seeing family that I had missed so much. But why didn't I feel elated. I was awarded most outstanding participant and I felt a sense of accomplishment but not excitement. I started missing the grilling of "PT", the sleepless nights and the rigid rules. How could this be when all I wanted to do initially was go home? Tears filled my eyes as the buses pulled into the gates. Bags packed and memories embedded in my mind, I hugged my friends and boarded the bus. With mixed emotions, I ended a chapter of my life.

As the bus came to a stop, I alighted from my seat to waiting hugs from my mom. She almost didn't recognize me since my toned lady like appearance hid the girl she once knew. The routine of "camp life" was still thick in my system, and adjusting to "normal life" became extremely difficult for me. The hours passed slowly, but the activities played like a broken record in my head. Day broke and I anxiously went outside to do my "PT." I relayed my camp experience to my family, much to their amusement. Night two came and went and sleep evaded me even more. I started to notice that the area where the penicillin injection was administered was red and swollen. The person in the mirror stared back at me and I didn't recognize her. "Mom my teeth are falling out" I yelled. It's the middle of the night girl go to sleep" said mom. I became afraid and crawled in the corner of the bed. As tears ran down my face, and sobs became louder, I heard footsteps getting closer. "What's the problem" asks mom. "Sleep with me please" I begged. "You are not a child anymore, so you need to stop the nonsense" said mom. And the click of the lights brought on a new reality. All my life I had never been afraid to sleep by myself and I couldn't understand why my mind was going at a pace that I couldn't control. I overheard my parents talking in their room. Dad was concerned with my strange behavior and asked mom to take me to the doctor. Morning could not have come soon enough. Mom asked me to get ready so she could take me to the doctor. A neighbor had told mom about a new doctor in town and she decided to take me there. Upon examination, the doctor explained that I was having an allergic reaction to the penicillin injection so I should ensure that I don't take any medication containing penicillin. "Rest and medication should take care of this" he said while writing the prescription. He had prescribed those small "white pills" that calms the nerves and sleep was my best friend for the next few days.

A week had passed and I started to feel like my usual self again. The physical activities had given me new confidence, and I day dreamed about my new job and couldn't wait until Monday morning to start. We were told to report to the to the local office which was located at the neighboring town Community Center. This building also housed the a government agency which deals with various aspects of community and social issues. I was thrilled to know that I was placed at that agency since it was a stone's throw away from my home. My first day was uneventful as I focused on learning the paper pushing job. As my responsibilities grew, so did my leadership abilities. Before long, I was asked to administer the affairs of the said program for that region. My willingness to take on any task and eagerness to learn new things gave me an advantage. It was difficult for anyone to tell my age at a glance. At 16 I displayed maturity beyond my years coupled with the fact that I was 5'11" and full figured. At the end of the six months (work experience), the organization could decide if they wanted to hire the participant full time. I was fortunate to be asked to stay. I was super excited to be able to earn since I had plans of going to college. I discussed my college prospects with my parents and they were pleased with my decision but were not able to support me financially. Undeterred, I wrote down my plans and told whoever asked that I was attending college that September.

One of the benefits was paying 50% of tuition for tertiary education, granted that a high standard of no less than a "B" is maintained. Jerusalem Moravian College had recently started their Associates Degree in Hospitality, Entertainment and Tourism, and I had my eyes on it. As I ascended the hills of Gibralter, a myriad of emotions bombarded my mind. The reality of a dream come through hit hard and tears of joy ran down my cheeks. I sat through the 30 minutes ride in public transportation and tried adjusting my mind to the everyday commute I needed to do for three years. One thing I knew for sure was that I wasn't going to quit. I dropped off the required documents for matriculation into the program at the administrative office and went home to await "the call." The anticipation was almost hard to bear. Two days came and went. I wondered if they had accepted me since I was barely 16 years old. A week came and went and no phone calls. I made sure to lie in wait for the mail man daily while I kept the phone nearby. After two weeks the mail man delivered a number of letters which I collected. There were six people living in the household and with enthusiasm, I skimmed through the pile. It appeared as if everybody else got a mail except me. Patiently I checked the names on the envelops until I came down to the last one. With a big sigh of relief, I nervously ripped open the envelop. "Dear Ms..." it read. "We are pleased to inform you that you have been accepted into our Associates Degree Program in Hospitality, Entertainment and Tourism Management... I skipped down to the tuition cost and my jaws dropped to the floor. I had no idea how I would afford college since my parents had already told me that they could not afford it. That weekend, on my usual visit to my parents' house, I broke the news to them with mixed emotions. Happiness was short lived as discussions of funding quickly took over and uncertainty was high. I needed $65k to complete the first year, and then based on my grades, the National Youth Service Program would start to pay. At 16 years old and living on a stipend of $600 per week, there were no savings. The college had asked for a deposit of $35k before a payment plan could be arranged. Undeterred, I prayed for a miracle. The deadline for the monies was fast approaching. My dad was a farmer who made his livelihood off cow, goats, sugar cane and ground provision. On a hunch, I decided to go visit him just to clear my head. He told me that he had sold one of his cows and had 25k to assist me. It was Friday afternoon and the banks closed earlier than usual. Monday was orientation day at school and I would need to present my proof of payment in order to be admitted. Realizing that I may not reach on time, I still decided to head to the bank. As I slipped through the door, the security guard turned the key for close of business. I waited to get to the teller and would not feel relieved until I had my receipt in my hand. $10k short, but better than none I thought. Stressful as it may be, a phase in a chain of events that would lead to fulfilling my life's ambitions had begun. The anxiety of college preparation made the days seem shorter and Monday came without hesitation. Amidst confidence and faith, I approached the admissions officer with my receipt. $25k was all I had and I managed to hatch an agreement to complete payment by the end of the school year.

With my usual friendly disposition, I scouted the strange faces for someone to welcome me. "Hi my name is Ger, you can call me Lisa" said a warm voice from behind. I peeped over my shoulder and was greeted with a handshake and a smile. We spoke about our backgrounds and the start of a new friendship was in sight. My day seemed less abstruse now that I had someone to share the new experience with. We were enrolled in different programs, but her friendship was a welcomed asset. The first few days were almost another "camp" experience. I wasn't a "boarder," but all first-year students had to stay on campus for the two-week orientation. The Student Council body oversaw the activities, and as part of the "initiation" everyone had to go through "grubbing." This practice I later discovered was also supported by the school's administration. My grandfather had told me about what to expect of college life and I swore not to comply. He had only attended grade school, heard stories from his son when he was at the university. It was bad enough to have to wear a 2'x2' cardboard sign around your neck with your title being "fresher", but at the end of week two, there would be a "fresher concert" parading all new students in their costumes (made of either cardboard, plastic bags or newspaper). By this time, the entire faculty and staff as well as the school body would have resumed and often, would be in attendance. As the days creped on, I took note of the requests of the leadership and adamantly refused to be humiliated. My strong spirited protest landed me in the vice principal's office. I wasted no time in informing the vice principal that the type of humiliation that students were subjected to, was not a part of the curriculum, and that I was not a willing participant. Numerous meetings and threats followed, but I stood my ground. I demanded to be refunded my tuition so I could find another institution that didn't tolerate this nonsense, all the while hoping that they wouldn't reverse my tuition arrangements because of my insubordination. There were a few other students who shared my views on this matter so "the march of the titans" continued. Concert day came and I decided to offer my rendition of a Celine Dion classic attired in my floor length formal dress and 4" heels. The Student Council president was furious. Chapel time was a fixture each morning as the school was a Moravian institution. Monday morning was no different except the defiance of five students headed by me, generated a detention list that was read aloud itemizing "offenses." After devotion, we were summoned to a meeting with the principal and the Student council body. We were asked to perform in the devotion the next day since we refused to follow the guidelines. The quick thinker that I was banded with the small group and decided to comply this time with something they would never forget. As we rehearsed the short skit, I thought about the possible consequences.......maybe expulsion. I played the part of the Student Council president, who was a short heavy set woman who looked very masculine and behaved like she was a regiment sergeant. Tuesday morning came and we waited for our "act" to be called on stage. The Student council president stood up and explained the "punishment" to the audience. I heard the satisfaction in her voice that she finally got us where she wanted us. As I debut my role, the new students started cheering me on. Before we could complete the script, the entire 3rd year group and the student council body walked out of the church hall. With broad smiles and a thumbs up, we walked to the bathroom to change into our uniforms. "We need an apology" they shouted. The vice principal stood in awe as she watched me strut to my class. The days that followed presented relentless pursuits for action against me, but undeterred and focused, I continued my journey. Time healed the wound I had left behind and anger turned into respect from my antagonists. As the distractions died, the class group members got to know me better and before long we were a tight nit small band of 4 – Kaye, Nessa. Lia and JT.

I had the option to live on campus but decided against it because I'd rather my own bed and space. I decided however to try it for a few weeks to see if I liked it. I shared a dorm with my college mates. We were told not to cook in the dorm rooms, but of course, that didn't apply to us. Money was really tight and whatever we could whip up on the hotplate was good enough for us. One night we pulled out the hot plate and started on our rice and mackerel meal. We cooked the rice first because it took the longer of the two. As soon as we started on frying up the mackerel, I saw the Dean heading down the corridor. Whenever we were cooking, on person would stay on the outside to make sure the course was safe. We hid the pots under the twin bunk beds and proceeded to finish what was left of the air freshener so the mackerel scent was not overwhelming. We hurriedly sat on the step as if nothing had happened and chatted with her. As soon as she left, I let go my breath and continued my cooking.

Year one approached its final stretch and the tuition stood in front of me like a brick wall. I didn't have any idea where to turn and I feared dropping out of school. I didn't expect to dry up my parents' meager source of income, and I didn't have a fairy god mother, or even a sugar daddy – or so I thought. A list of names was read in the devotion for a meeting with the vice principal. Of Course, my name headed that list. I attended the meeting without hesitation as I was curious about the options I could explore. No compromises – pay by the end of the month and get the "pass" so we can sit exams. My mind went in a spin. I was actively preparing for exams I may never be able to do. How could I be on my desired path and have my dreams dashed in the blink of an eye? Two weeks isn't enough time to find all that money. But, I remembered a commitment I made to settle up before year end and I quietly slipped out to make my way home. That night, sleep disappeared like a scorned lover. My whirlwind romance with destiny seemed too near its end and rivers of tears flowed down my cheeks. I prayed between sobs – "Lord please help me." I decided to complete the classes and maybe I could get to do the exam when I can afford to pay for it. The next morning, I brushed myself off, washed my tears away and went to class. My friends noticed that I wasn't my normal self so I told them what had happened. Their encouragement was well appreciated but it didn't calm the fears. Class went on uneventfully until after lunch. The lecturer announced that all students will be required to present "exam passes" from the bursar's office before being able to enter the examination room. The silence was deafening. Plan B went out the window and there were no other plan. My ship had hit block ice at sea and was now taking in water. Humiliated and disappointed, I bid my friends goodbye and headed home. I never saw myself as a charity case and my pride would not allow me to beg. A glimmer of hope was all I needed to go on. Between sobs, I removed my books from my bedside table and packed them in the corner on the carpeted floor. I stared at them for a moment and covered them with a towel so I wouldn't be reminded of my failure. Tears were my lullaby while I prayed for sleep to visit me.

I had been corresponding with a male friend I had met through Lisa. I enjoyed the conversations, and he was always encouraging me along. That night, I laid in bed scrolling through my mind trying to find an answer since I couldn't sleep. The phone rang, but I wasn't in the mood to talk so I ignored it. But it kept ringing. After a while, I decided to answer. "Hello" in the most depressed tone possible. "Why haven't you been taking my calls? I've been trying to reach you all day" he said. "I am not feeling well." "What's the matter?" "I'm going to drop out of college because I can't afford it right now." "Are you out of your mind? How much do you owe them?" "$40K." "By when do you need to pay it?" "It's already overdue." My heart started racing as I began realizing where the conversation was going. "OK I'm going to call you tomorrow when I send it. Don't shut me out when you have issues because I want to help you." I stood in shock as tears welded up in my eyes. I couldn't respond because I was in awe. I started to question myself and his motives. What is he going to ask for in return? As the conversation ended, I consoled myself with a "thank you" prayer and my faith in God had been restored.

A performance report had to be submitted to the program headquarters so that monies can be disbursed for tuition. Confident but anxious, I collected my first-year report. "Excellent student" it read. I punched the air as I glanced over "A." I couldn't wait to submit my "trophy." Tears of joy filled my eyes as I accepted a job offer from the program directors to work at one of their locations as house mother for the summer. I had been familiar with the job and was elated for the opportunity to give back as well as earn some well needed money. My first assignment was in St. Mary, a place I had only seen on TV. The three-hour journey took me out of familiar territory and brought me to a whole new experience. I trusted my ability to adapt, and with a few deep breaths I reached deep inside of me for that "brave girl" my grandfather once told me about. What could have prepared an 17 year old for a job as a "house mother?" I had only been a participant a year and a half ago and the experience changed everything about me. So how does one treat with a situation as this? Do I present myself as ironclad or nurturing? I'm not even a mother. Most if not all the participants are older than me. What did they see in me to be confident that I could perform this job? As I conversed with myself, my grandfather's voice became louder in my ear – "rise to the challenge and be brave." After all, my deportment was that of maturity and charisma. The experience proved to be extremely enriching as I learned how to manage, adapt and respond to various situations, many of which I have never encountered before or even imagined. I taught things I didn't know and wasted no time learning from everyone. The days turned into weeks, and before long, I was saying my goodbyes.

The close of one fulfilling journey and the start of another brought new excitement. As I counted my blessings, I made my way to the main office of the NYS to pick up my check since I had submitted a sterling college report for the end of the first year. I had saved up enough money to pay half of the second year's tuition and my parents were always supplementing my income whenever they can afford to do so. Second year felt more comfortable for me and I hoped that I would have a smoother one. Prayers were always a major part of my routine. I grew up in the Seventh Day Adventist church where my grandmother was a staunch member. Every Sabbath, my siblings and I would have to follow mama to a small church located in the adjoining district.

Sometimes we took public transportation, but more often than not, we walked. The approximately three-mile journey would not be as hard had it not been through sweltering 98 degrees under the sky's canopy. What mama said was law, so no sense in trying to back out. After a while though, I looked forward to going to church to enjoy the time away from home. I was always the adventurous type and loved new experiences. Mom and Dad were not church goers, but my dad grew up in the Adventist church and occasionally attended the Moravian church during his childhood. So, we would sometimes visit the Moravian church which was just a stone's throw away. Teenage years had set in and church was no longer a priority. However, I never forgot where my strength came from.

Thick as thieves, we were four girls enjoying college life: Vanessa had migrated to the USA and Kerry and I did what college girls do. Our adventures took us to many parties in and around the surrounding, as most college students do. One of the most memorable ones for me was a college party in the lunch room hosted by the third-year group. Although we were second year students, we were allowed to attend. Alcohol was allowed and no one asked for IDs. I was there with Kaye who also enjoyed a few drinks. At the time, I didn't drive and she had the connections to a ride home. So, I proceeded to purchase my "Appleton and Pepsi" combo. I enjoyed every moment of it and the music felt like magic in my "tipsy" state, or so I thought. I needed to go to the restroom which was located on the outside of the building. As soon as the night air hit me, I felt as if I was cornered by confusion and imbalance. I was stoned- drunk-high on the "rum tree" and that's as much as I remembered. The next day I woke up in my bed naked. I shuffled around to find my clothes, because I really needed to go to the bathroom. As I ran towards the passage half naked, my stomach reminded me that I had not treated it well the night before and was paying the price now. My sisters were getting ready for the beach and I was a fixture on the toilet. For the next two days, I had to remain close to the toilet, unable to eat or drink. I decided against going to the doctor because I was ashamed to explain the reason for my condition. So the home remedies were my only option – salt, salt, and more salt. I thought I needed to find out how I got home and why I was naked so I called Kaye. She was laughing so hard as soon as she answered the phone. "You laughed all the way home and I made sure you were home and inside before I left" she said. I was relieved because I didn't want to be the victim of sexual abuse, especially as a result of my actions. That act of kindness further cemented our friendship.

Third year was challenging and fun to say the least. Expectations were high as I was now on the home stretch. I had received the 50% tuition form the NYS as promised and made arrangements with the administration to pay the remainder prior to final exams. I had my usual summer job and had managed to save some money, but expenses for school were exorbitant (for a poor girl) and I could not afford to pay the tuition. I attended classes and fulfilled all the requirements for the program up to the point of the semester break. As usual, a "pass" in the form of a signed slip from the bursar's office was required to do exams and most recently, it was introduced for class attendance. It was now time to go home and relax until I could afford to complete my finals. Lecturers were instructed not to allow "outliers" to attend class and I knew I was on that list. I bathed in my pity. "Why me Lord? Why do I have to struggle so much just to get an education while others have the opportunity and waste it?"

My body clock alarmed and I peeped through the window with one eye still asleep. No reason to get up, I thought as I couldn't go to class. I turned on my back, drew the covers and slept in till mid-day. By then, the worms in my stomach started misbehaving and I had to respond. Food felt like an enemy and a try at my favorite, curry chicken and white rice, proved futile. The bed became my refuge, at least for now. I decided to visit my parents since I had all the time in the world. I was very considerate of them as I knew that their livelihood couldn't afford tuition, and furthermore, they had already given me what they could afford. So I chatted with them all the while leading them to believe that I was off school just for the day. My mom was a very jovial person and by the time I was ready to go home, my spirit was lifted.

As the darkness chased away the daylight, I decided to relax and watch a movie. The phone rang and I answered very little enthusiasm. I didn't want to be disturbed and I thought about hanging it up. "What's up girl" said the woman on the line. "I'm ok" I fibbed. "Everyone was asking for you today including Mrs. Taylor. She says you are to come back to class and she was upset that you choose not to" said Vee. "I won't be humiliated, I prefer to sit out until I can afford my way" I snapped. "I'm just telling you what she said. I see you're not in the mood to talk, good night." Without another word said, she hung up the phone. I thought about my response and really wanted to apologize for snapping at my friend. I steered at the phone briefly and slammed it on the bed. But I couldn't shake Mrs. T's request. Suppose I get caught in class and suspended, I thought. I decided to sleep on it.

The next morning, I woke up early. Revived and rested, I strutted into the bathroom to take a shower. My appetite had returned so I made myself some breakfast. As I ate, I made a plan for my day – which included sleep, sleep and more sleep. My pride wouldn't allow me to be humiliated. After breakfast, I sat on the porch overlooking the street to enjoy some morning breeze. I watched the neighborhood kids going off to school and waved as they greeted me. The sound of a car in the distance caught my attention. It looked familiar. I was right; it was Mrs. T's car. Mrs. T was one of her lecturers who lived in the community where I grew up. She alighted from her car and waited with one foot inside the driver's door. Mrs. T was tall, dark skinned and beautiful and had the sweetest soft but stern voice that anyone could ever have. "Are you crazy" she shouted in a loud whisper. "How could you come this far and decide to quit now. I won't allow you to do that." Overwhelmed by emotions, nose burning, and muscles engaged me to fight back the tears; I responded, "I'm not going to let them humiliate me." "Go and put on your uniform. I'm not leaving you this morning" said Mrs. Taylor. I took that as a command and suddenly realized that this was a fight I couldn't win so I complied. Class went on uneventful and after my sessions ended, Mrs. T told me to meet her in town the next day.

Uniformed and eager, I waited at the taxi stand for Mrs. T. I thought that she was going to take me to school. She also taught at the High school near town and don't usually do morning classes at the colle. The bluish sedan turned the corner and smiles greeted me. "Go in the bank and pay your tuition and go to school" she said as she handed me an envelope. Before I could look up, or even respond, she drove off. Tears cascaded down my face as I opened the envelope. Nervous and excited, I counted the bills. I attempted to walk across the street to the bank, but my legs needed more time to stop shaking. The magnitude of what just happened was hard to comprehend. Was this a loan? But how am I going to pay her back? I don't have a job and the little I get from my parents is just for food and transportation. She didn't even discuss the terms with me. When does she want me to repay her? Questions drove up and down my mind until there was a traffic jam. A soft stern voice said "go into the bank and pay your tuition and go to school." I pulled myself together, walked into the bank and hurriedly boarded a taxi. With my head held high, I stepped into the administrative office and handed the receptionist the receipt. With pass in hand, I boldly walked into the classroom smiling from ear to ear. No explanations or excuses to be given to anyone because guardian angels weren't meant to be broadcast. The page has turned and the future beckons. I now have a new challenge to succeed, not only for my parents, but my "guardian angel".

The days went by rather quickly as I burned the midnight oil. I'd perfected a pattern of study that saw me through my first and second years and I was now running on auto pilot. I slept the first part of the night through to 2am and then studied all the way to daylight, jumped in the shower and head off to the exams. I would often break for a snack and some music and then get back on course.

Before you knew it, I was preparing for graduation. Mom had gotten a visa to visit the United States of America, and was excited to take back a graduation dress and shoes for me. All graduates had to wear white dresses and mine was perfect. The shoes however didn't fit because mom underestimated my size 11 feet. I jokingly told mom "I'm a big girl so little feet wouldn't wear well on me." After a good laugh, they went shoes shopping for the big day. Nineteen and graduating college with an "honors" Associates Degree was quite an accomplishment in my mind. I was cognizant though that my journey had just begun and that I need to keep "the plan" in mind. I was the first of my siblings to graduate college and was proud walking that corridor. My paternal grandma had come from the USA just for the event and I felt even more extraordinary. Although I enjoyed college life, I was happy that the curtains came down on that chapter. Already, I was planning on job hunting since I had no idea where I would get any money had I decided to continue graduate school.

The days following graduation were all about enjoyment. I had been studying for three years, and didn't feel free enough to actually rest my mind from the money worries. Although the partying on the weekend was a part of my college routine, it felt different because I didn't have to go to school on Monday.

It was approaching the end of August, and I had aspirations of working in the hotel sector. Although I was employed, the job was not my ideal one and I was determined to succeed at whatever I do. I continued to send out applications to hotels in the north coast. I checked the post office daily for responses, but none came. I did follow up calls – "no vacancy" they said. I kept searching because I wasn't a quitter. Days turned into anxious weeks and I rummaged through my mind to see who I could ask for a job. My current job wasn't my ideal job, so I continued my search.

The "continuing college" idea from my "prince charming" came at an opportune time. He offered to pay the tuition to do the teacher education course and the deal was on. Preparation for college again was an awesome experience since I now had someone to help me financially. This made him even more attractive to me because he empowered me.

Friday was an unusually lazy day for me. I had completed all the necessary preparation for college and decided to relax on my love seat. The phone blared in the background as I dozed off. I gathered enough strength to stretch across to grab the receiver. "Hello" I said half asleep. "Good afternoon. My name is Mrs. Witter from the Human Resource department of Couples resort. May I speak to Ms. Thompson?" said the very polished female voice on the other side of the line. I sat up quickly and pulled my thoughts together. I had been waiting for this call for months, and look at the timing. College was all I think about now, and it wouldn't be feasible to accept a job that's approximately three hours from where I lived. "This is her" I answered. "We have reviewed your application and would like to offer you a junior housekeeping supervisor position at our prestigious resort" said Mrs. Witter. I was excited; however, it was short lived. "Thanks for the opportunity Mrs. Witter, I would love to. But I've already enrolled in college and would not be able to accept the position" I stuttered. Mrs. Witter further explained that they were interested in putting me in their training program because they were looking for people like me to be a part of the organization. I felt humbled by the offer but my eyes were dead set on college. I immediately called my friend Sher, (who had been my "cumbaya" since the beginning of high school) to tell her about my conversation. Sher was a very supportive and loyal confidant. We shared all the "ups and downs" in our lives and were never judgmental. Her advice was always welcomed and we respected each other's' opinion. That night, I went to sleep feeling appreciated and looked forward to the days when employers would come searching for me.

Chapter

Heavenly Visit

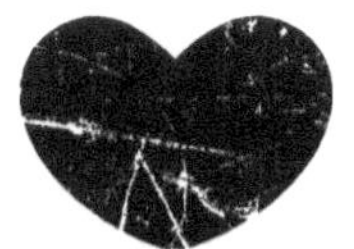

The sun peeped through the thick curtains as I rolled over lazily. It was the weekend and so I kept my eyes closed so as not to wake them up. No work to go to so sleep was in order. My stomach didn't agree with the plan though. By now, the sun was high in the sky and the heat warned that mid-day was approaching. I dragged myself out of bed and sat on the bed's edge in order to get my day together in my mind. Laundry, cleaning, cooking… but they will get done whenever. I had not gotten "the phone call", but I prayed for patience. I hung out with my sisters between chores, but a part of me couldn't shake the thought of him. Is he going to call? Is he thinking about me as much as I am thinking about him? Loneliness wrapped me so tight; I could barely breathe. Why do I feel lonely and my sisters are in the same space as I am? As I excused myself and walked to my room, my thoughts of him made me miss hearing him even more. Impatience got the better of me and I found myself with the phone in hand dialing his number. "Hello I wanted to hear you so I called. Are you OK?" I said nervously. "Yes" he said. "I was going to call you because I wanted to hear you as well." I released a loud sigh. Confirmation! My anxiety turned into major happiness. He was thinking about me too. Half hour seemed to go by so quickly and by the end of the conversation, I had enough energy to take me through my chores.

I looked forward to the sisters' weekly Sunday eat out. The Bakery restaurant was the place to be on a Sunday evening as Sunday was declared a "no cooking" day. The strides of three beautiful young ladies along that twenty-minute walk, often attracts a lot of attention from passersby; some wanting to "give us a ride." Youthful exuberance bursting through our being and dressed to kill, we strolled down the street just to have a meal and return home. Tripe and bean were among our favorite dish, but the time spent together was even more fun. It was hard not to notice us so everyone who came into the restaurant that day felt the need to comment. We bathed in the compliment. Sher sometimes joined us when she could get away from her parents. They went to church on Sundays, and she would rarely be allowed to skip out. She was quiet and shy, but we were like peas in a pod. The stipend we made from our jobs was enough to spoil us with one outing per week. Sunday was our special time and we looked forward to that getaway that few would find significant.

The work week went by uneventfully. With each passing day I marked an "X" on my calendar as I counted down to the weekend. He had promised to take me out. As the curtains closed on the work week, the butterflies in my stomach multiplied and did their happy dance. After a cold shower, I carefully creamed the length of her 5'11" cappuccino skin. The mist of my favorite perfume filled the air as I searched my beige fabric closet for the perfect outfit. It suddenly dawned on me that I had not heard from him yet. I glanced at the small faithful clock on the make shift bed side table and then starred at the phone beside it. It was 9pm and I prayed: "Lord please let him show up." The ticking of the clock seemed louder than usual as I lay on my back deep in thought. The phone rang and I quickly grabbed the receiver. "Time to get dressed" I said as I picked up the phone. My happy feet danced as I enhanced my perfectly symmetrically balanced cheeks with light powder and some earth tone eye shadow to my tiny brown eyes. I accessorized my classy look with gold jewelry and spun around one last time to make sure everything was in place.

The lights pitched off my window and I knew it was time to ride off into the night with my "prince Charming". With shoulders perfectly straight and feet aligned one step in front of the other, I walked toward the car and into his waiting arms. The embrace was so intense. Nothing else mattered now. His whispers of compliments filled my ears and I basked in the moment. As I opened my eyes I realized that the sky's smile also celebrated my joy. The moon and stars have never looked as bright as they played across the sky's floor. "Let's go baby" he said as he escorted me to the passenger side of the car. I eased out of his embrace and floated to the seat. We were like magnet and steal as we slowly drove towards Spur Tree Hill. Anywhere with him is ok, I thought. The conversation was enough to set the tone for the night. The level of comfort between us was magical. The steep hills of Spur Tree took on new meaning as the car came to a stop in an area almost on the edge of the road overlooking St. Churchill. As he parked close to the unfenced area, I felt my heart tug at my chest. He asked me to accompany him outside and I readily agreed. The beauty of the lights in the distance was breathtaking, and although I had seen it before in passing, it felt as if a red carpet had been rolled out just for me. He held me from behind in an embrace that was to die for. His soft hands wasted no time in caressing me. Tingles filled my body and I fought in futility to hide the shivering. As we continued our "getting to know each other" session, the noise of passing traffic drifted away and drowned in whispers of love. The heavy winds occasionally disturbed the moments and I knew it must be past midnight. "Are you cold baby" he whispered. He asked again and I realized that my mouth didn't say what my mind was thinking. I wasn't sure if it was the wind or the "moment" that caused me to shake and become warm by his embrace, all at the same time. The kissing intensified to the point of breathlessness. He paused long enough to ask me "would you go somewhere with me baby." "Yes" I responded. And before I knew it, the Nissan Stanza was blazing in all her glory towards Nashville. I sat in a reclined position with my eyes closed, still savoring the moments. I felt the car slowed and then turned. Curiosity got the better of me so I slowly let the light into my eyes. He drove through a side street and I raised my head to see where we were. I glanced at the fully lit sign by the gate. Sunset View Hotel it read, and as the security guard hoisted the iron bar, I quickly sat up and checked my clothes to ensure that I was decent. "I'll be back" he said as he alighted from the car towards the reception area. Every move he made turned me on a little more. "Go up the stairway and across the hall, and room 201 is on the left." Said the receptionist whose desk was only a few feet away from where he parked. Anticipating his return, I stepped out of the car and gazed in the sky just to check if she was still smiling at me. And sure enough, the stars squinted back. The walk was short but memorable. I felt as if I was about to be knighted. The moon walked beside me all the way down the passage to room 201. He nervously opened the door and checked his domain. He was an alert person and ensured that it was safe for us before we went in. As I sat on the bed, he tilted my head and planted a wet kiss on my waiting lips.

"Relax baby I'll be back in a few minutes" he said as he closed the door behind him.

Disappointed and amused I flung myself on the bed. The minutes felt like they were going super slow as the clock ticked like a lazy army. 10 minutes seemed like an hour and discomfort began to set in. My mind wondered. How dare him lock me in a hotel room in the middle of the night and leave me here. Before I could move on to the next thought, the sound of turning keys and an open door brought me back to reality. "Where have you been" I asked. "To pray baby, my dream came through and I had to make sure it was real" he said. I couldn't believe what he said. But before I could enjoy a good laugh, we picked up right where we left off. Time stood still as he moved his long fingers down the length of my spine. His lips travelled slowly on my neck and I felt as if I would explode. Mesmerized and captivated, I responded hungrily yet passionately. We made music such that a world class symphony had nothing on us. "I've never been loved this way" I whispered between grasps for air. "I'm speechless" he responded. We breathlessly fell into each other's arms and were soon stolen by sleep.

BLOOMING ROSE

Her lady is like a rose

Waiting to release beauty

Deep to her core pink

Tucked and asleep under her mink

Never quick to expose

Because she values that beautiful rose

Time alone can reveal

And only the right one can steal

She's yearning to see the sun

Feel the heat but she won't run

Taste the gentle sips

Just before the wind smothers her tips

Go ahead

Sprout her buds

She'll prove her love

Make her one

With the heavens up above

The bees will pitch and tease

But that won't appease

Her need to release sweet perfumes

Let the air rise

In front of her eyes

And melody escape

Slowly

Not in a haste

Uncover her folds

Be attentive to her pose

Break that mold

To discover peerless beauty

She'll open wide

Underneath the skies

Be sure to protect her

So her petals won't die

With gentle strides

And a kiss goodnight

She'll be fine to weather the night

He shuffled in the dark amongst his clothes. "What is it" I whispered half asleep. "I'm looking at the time. It's 2 o'clock and I need to take you home." I didn't care if anyone was worried about me. All I knew is that I rubbed my genie and it granted my wish. He guided me to the shower stall and proceeded to run the water so it would be just the right temperature for me while he held me tight enough to keep my knees from buckling under my weight. As the water warmed, so did his embrace. He slipped out of my reciprocating embrace momentarily to look at me. I could get lost in those eyes. They were mysterious, but I could at least see fulfillment in them. He mentioned that my body felt like velvet and he couldn't keep his hands off me. Little did he know that I was thinking the same thing. He lathered my body with his bare hands while gently kissing me through streams of water. Why did this have to end? I thought as he toweled my 5 feet 11 inches of melanin. He reminded me in between kisses that there would be a lot more nights like this. I softly nodded and smiled in agreement.

The tone of the journey home was relaxed and fulfilling. As the moon said goodnight and the stars wrote our names across the sky, I melted in his arms one more time and reluctantly slipped into my door.

The passion of the night had drained me and I soon drifted off into "la la land".

Morning appeared to appear quicker that it did on other days. I rolled over to greet the sun peeping through my window. My head wondered off to the events of last night, and I decided to put pen to paper…

I LOVE YOU!

I

That's ME – all of me. Every part that's dripping with nervous emotions only for you.

The part that only I can feel. The place in my chest that doesn't feel real. But this is me.

LOVE

What is love? I'm not sure but it creates a feeling inside my body that's indescribable – but I know I'm in LOVE.

YOU

You are my special person. The strong yet gentle physique, the soothing voice, those beautiful eyes, the safe embrace, the beard on my face – I LOVE YOU!

Love Like This

I've loved before

Or so I thought

But I've never felt love until this morning

Amidst the gentle kisses stretches and yawning

Draping my heart to the sound of birds calling

Together they spoke to me in a foreign tone

Of feelings only experienced on a movie screen

I've seen beautiful sunsets before

The ones that pitched effervescent hues on the distant shores

And makes my body tingle for more

But I've never seen the sun and moon dance on the sky's floor

Or match make among majestic clouds and knock at heaven's door

So I'm trying to keep score

Of cosmic encounters with the one I adore

I've seen caterpillars turn into butterflies

Protected by their cocoon sitting on a tree branch high

And with time morphs into one ready to fly

But I've never seen beauty like the look in your eyes

When you wrap your arms around me tight

Providing all the love and support I desire

To fly away high in the sky like a butterfly

Never to return to my chrysalis cause together we'll fly

I've loved before

I've experienced this illusive thing

With all the heartbreak it brings

And all the pain and suffering

But in spite of the head and heart wrestling

I still want to wear your ring

Then give Andrew a few siblings

Cause after this I'll never love again

Uncensored Love

They say it is strong and sweet

That it will be the lamp that guides your feet

To experience heaven on earth

You must embrace its very girth

When floods around you rage

It will be the raft on which you float

They say it's pure and generous

For it freely flows from the honey pot

When the spoils of life are few

It will surely carry you through

And though it may sometimes be small and selfish

There's always sweet in the roses

It stirs the soul and churns beauty

Calls the blood into your veins

Builds castles out of dreams

And mends the broken pieces well

Test its strength and you will see

Cast uncensored love like a spell

49

CLOUD 9

I need a memory of you in my bed

Right at the place where I lay my head

So that on the days when there's no one to hold me like you do

I can return to that place to calm my fears

I need to make memories that no one can delete

Store them in my bank with only me holding the keys

With hopes that deposits exceed withdrawals

And there's no bankruptcy or fraudulent trials

I'll always treasure room 201

That's the place where our spirits mingled and souls wove unbreakable bonds

The pain of separation was intense for days

But I'll allow the heart to do what it do

Today I desire your special touch and I sure hope I'm not asking too much

Just slow caresses along the length of my being

Make sure your finger is my mouth so I don't scream

I need your passion to overflow even if only in my dreams

I don't care if sweet memories taunt me

My personal space must have an experience I can replay when I want
you

Let's create a special place angels envy

Only with better music above cloud 9

BEAUTIFUL

When I call you beautiful

It's not because I see your melanin skin that so smooth with the right
tint

Or that smile that exposes those strong teeth I'd love to feel gently
gripping my flesh

It's not even about that perfectly aligned salt and pepper beard I long
to feel on my face

It's because you are the one who fuels my dreams

When I call you beautiful

It's because you're thoughtful and respectful

Your mannerisms are graceful

Head to toe your distinctive style makes me want to go wild

But though you know you're admirable

Your humility blows my mind

I hope the next person that calls you beautiful

Knows that I saw all of you and I hope they meant it the way I do

That I saw your soul and it made me feel whole

Every time I think about you I imagine a garden

With colors blended and fragrance inspired

Cause I'd wear you until you're tired

But I'll always call you beautiful my love just the way you are.

YOUR FRIENDSHIP

There's something in your friendship that soothes my fears

Calms my mind and chases away my tears

There's something that's good for rainy days

When life happens and the sun refuse to come out to play

There something about your friendship

The unselfish advice that you freely give

The experiences shared even those very few have lived

The gratitude of life and love and blessings

That speaks of your heart reminiscing

Many friendships in life I've enjoyed

Some have ended leaving others annoyed

Ours have ticked all the boxes

Causing me tranquility amongst unrest

And I'm just loving our little nest

So I look towards a future with care

Knowing that what we share is very rare

Never will I try to compare

For there's only one of you that's kind and true

To Our friendship I'll forever be glued

SOMEONE SOMEWHERE

There's someone somewhere

that captures my attention

My heart dances to his sweet melodic rhythm

He's a rent free tenant

In my head everyday

All I know is that there is someone somewhere who makes my soul
glad

Butterflies dance to his voice

They follow his Glowing light

Just like an angel when he's ready he takes his flight,

Bright smiles light up the dark

That makes my spirit light,

There's someone somewhere who fits me perfect like a glove.

Your presence cause me to feel

experience strange things

Knots, curls, daze, and intense enthusiasm,

Amazed by his strong built

yet gentle stature,

There's someone somewhere who satisfies every room of my head.

I think to set him free

but my heart clenches,

My belly burns though my body quenches

What do I do with all these

Crazy gut punches,

When that someone somewhere release my heart from his grip

Now I know that the heart is a separate being

Capable of flight or fight or even plight

But I man chose immense delight,

Wrapped in a package that looks just like you

So today I awake to thoughts of holding you

there's someone somewhere, and that someone is YOU!

LOVE

What is it about this thing called love?

When it's good it makes you fly high like a dove

Create butterflies even when there are no blooms falling from above

Bonds your heart your soul and everything else you'll shove

Think for a minute about this thing called love

Its newness illuminates the darkness like stadium bulbs

Decisions made fast to give each other all just like the lion and her cub

No thoughts of tomorrow in fact the next minute is a smudge

Then when poverty show up through the window love will jump

For this thing many have taken their last breath

Hurt pain and sorrow experienced and no hope except

When all expectations are not met

Load the barrel pull the trigger but you won't forget

That one who stirred your passion creating contractions reducing your
attention now you're dealing with contention

What do you know about this thing called love?

Is it just a feeling that you get when from the top boxes ticked and
what they taught is met

Or is the brain seeking comfort for a brain washed heart that's
stressed

Is it enough to sustain that bond you formed after Pandora's box
unveils itself

There's still so much mystery to this thing called love

When it's good it's great

Makes your heart melt and you forget you could ever hate

Anxiety and depression it will negate

Causing you a high wishing you'll always be in that state

What a beauty to behold with this thing called love

They say there are different versions of the same

I won't begin to mention any names

Take your time to find don't crash and burn like a plane

Or rush and crush little hearts don't even think to entertain

For there will be a great measure of disdain

A million years gone and more still to come there's still not enough
learned about this thing called love.

Soul Connection

I think I love him

Not only because of the way he softly caresses my cheeks with his beard or the wet kisses on my lips

It's not even about the movement of his loins when we're locked into a grind but god damn that blows my mind

I could close my eyes and get lost in his smile all day all night without even getting tired

I think our love liberates

The little moment we physically touch don't even mean as much as the constant connection of our minds

And when hearts and souls combine sensations unwind intimacy beyond space and time permeates the stratosphere creating an envelope in which you and I continue to develop apart but together

This electric connection has no need for dissension even though our spirits are free should we lose focus or get cross eyed then we possess the strength to perform strabotomy intricately correcting strabismic tendencies

I know I love him

We communicate in the realm of angels

Mind you the universe is our stage our hearts never want to be caged

We absorb each other like a sponge to water we engage

This heavenly concoction is more than rice and peas curry goat and roti escoveitch fish and bammy ackee and salt fish but it is soul food

When he stirs the pot the fragrance fills my being

And I know nothing can intervene

Distance between on islands in the seas fuels our passion until the next time our bodies reunite

LOST IN YOU

I am captivated by the way you talk

Colors dance in my head as the words stealthily leave your lips

My mind's amiss I lose track of time

One smile and my world goes in a spin

Baby I get lost in your words

Heaven opened up to the sound of your voice

Ushered me in with a gentle wind

Cords and notes so symphonic and divine

A perfect blend that makes my ear glad

Darling your voice transports me to a special place

Those arms that held my Years at bay

Also sheltered my heart's strong rays

Perfectly protecting every inch of my being

Warding off insecurities and boosting confidence within

Sweetheart your hug means everything

The perfect you only exist for me

When all of you speaks to all of me

The best part is already etched in time

Now we're forever intertwined

The truth is… I'm lost in you!

My Perfect You

When the wind blows It sprinkles your essence atop trees

Filling the air with fragrance that attracts not only bees

A special perfume that energize souls like mine

Only you and the wind can share the same divine

Like the rain you water every inch of my soul

A perfect mix that only you and the rain could fix

Protecting me from all the elements untold

Synchronizing our energies lasting until we're old

In your embrace lies everything and more

If time could stop so I can inhale you to my core

Expand my inner peace so loving you won't be a chore

And then lay in those safe arms now and forevermore

With you our future looks bright

We could dance all day into the night

When disappointments come then victory ignite

The same hand that comforts will celebrate when the time is right

FOREVER

Not life or death

Nor scheme well planned

Can ever snatch

Me from your hand

The one who steals

Remain subdued

Cause none was created quite like you

I'm free to live

Each day anew

All cares of life

Already withdrew

With outstretched arms

And smiles brand new

I now release my peace to you

That day we met

I'll never regret

The birds respond

With melodic duets

From life's first cry

To my final breath

Our hearts will remain closest

Forever is you

Forever is me

This is the power

That binds our destiny

Hell can't unleash

It's power is quelled

I'll stand with you forevermore

SOUL MATE

Our parents must have known

That when we're grown we'd be inseparable

They must have thought of us that moment their bodies touched

To create someone so imperfectly perfect

And though I wasn't your first choice

I want to be the last person you see late at night

I am one with you

You held me in every way

Even when my emotions were in a sway

In your arms I'm a strong tower

Nothing could penetrate your wall of fire around my heart

And the sky is too low a limit

To describe how high I'll fly when you're near me

The ocean isn't deep enough to gage the depth I'll go just to reach you

You complete me

Every inch of me says I love you

It's the way my brain danced at the sound of your voice

It's the raised hairs on my skin when you're near

It is impossible to ignore the effortless response of my hips to your
hands

They lock in a grind even before that's on your mind

I can't help but melt into your perfect chest

And hold my breath in your embrace

You are the love of my life

You're the spark in my eyes

The touch that warms my life

The gentle wind against my skin

I want to be better for me so I can be great for you

I see you just for who you are

With me You'll never need to disguise

And though it may come as a surprise

You are my soulmate!

Men Like You

Men like you are rarest gems

Rugged beauty deep within

Vivid hues radiating through

Of intense pleasure and satisfaction too

Men like you are among the few

Who heals wounds and make anew

Therapeutic in nature, who knew

That you would be that glue

Men like you create passion

That makes wildfires spread

Igniting bodies that once was dead

And keeps them warm in bed

Men like you cannot be tamed

Your energy is precious and wild

Pulsating across distant tides

Always by my side

Men like you I love to love

Cause you delight my senses and please my mind

The peace you bring will linger still

You're the sun that warms my day

SOMETHING

There's something about you that ease the tightness in my chest

Calms my racing heart and puts my mind at rest

There's something about my head being on your breast

That give me unspeakable joy and great happiness

There's something about the way your eyes lock with mine

Piercing my inner woman making me feel fine

A gentle rhythm of colors our hearts intertwine

This intricate dance only our soul can define

Whenever I stumble your love is my safety net

As sure as the tides on a summer's day getting my feet wet

My heart's pains seeped away in the midnight air

When that something you possess wraps me in its cozy nest

FIRE AND ICE

I love the way you melt me

Wrap me in your embrace and caress me

Slowly transform me into a flood

You're the fire to my ice

I just love the way you stir my tide

Let me flow from side to side

Until I begin to bubble and rise

You're the fire to my ice

You make my harmonies build

Play my strings till I begin to sing

Building symphonic bridges that join our worlds

You're the director of my orchestra

Oh what a tasty dish we make

When we choose to experiment with taste

Add the right ingredients to my mix

You're the pepper in my spice

When my parts come to a violent boil

You slowly take me down to simmer

Keep me warm till it's time to eat

Just before we both go to sleep

You're the fire to my ice!

FEEL MY LOVE

When around you there's only rain

And you feel nothing but pain

I would love to be the one you embrace

I'll make you feel my love

The world is a complicated place

Sometimes even knock you off your feet

Let me be the cushion on which you fall

Then pick you up so you could stand tall

When the shadows are too dark to see

And fear grips too tight to breathe

I'll be your blue skies to illuminate the dark

And dry your soul of all the pain

When your eyes' river floods your face

And it seems like there's no escape

I'll be the shoulder and I'll dry them my dear

Stay awhile and feel my love

77

When the stars in the skies are at peace

It's because they know my love won't leave

They'll serenade us while our bodies tease

I'll hold you till eternity then you'll feel my love

Fan My Flames

This fire I found isn't new

It was hidden deep inside of me

But one encounter with the air you blew

Ignited my dormant flames anew

I sought out soul stirring ties

Ones that will keep this fire alive

Some were only violent flames

That died quickly oh what a shame

I wasn't sure that when sparks flew

That this was just one of the familiar few

Trust that time will reveal its truth

But for now my flames burn into the night

It's in your warm embrace

Heartbeats that jumpstarts a slow pace

A language that my spirit comprehend

Cause you continue to fan my flames

When the night falls asleep

And the wintery mix starts to peep

Way past the dusk and morning dew

I hope my flames stay burning through

Aqua Blue

Aqua blue

Shining through

Radiant hues

Pitched anew

Lightly pitched

The waters lips

The sun's gentle kiss

Should never be missed

Oh morning rise

And bless my eyes

Let your warmth surround

My cold abode

Stir the bird's nests

Bring music to my chest

So I awake

To greet the day

The sand recede

From beneath my feet

Her waves crash hard

Against my limbs

I feel them move

As you strum the beat

Oh aqua blue

I am renewed

I Believe

I believe in butterflies

The ones that come alive

When you spread my thighs

Those that tickle my innermost

Raising my passion to the uttermost

And making me float from coast to coast

I believe in butterflies

I believe in forevermore

A life with you never feels like a chore

Cause you break my fall

Give me your all

Pick me up and make me stand tall

I want to be the yin to your yang

I believe in forevermore

I believe in you and me

You're my king and I your queen

Allowing no other love to get between

Protecting our hearts and on each other lean

Be your tower of strength

Together we'll be a power team

I believe in you and me

THEY SAY

They say we'll never cross

That this sea is too wide to pass

And this mountain too high to scale

They say we'll be old and gray

Before our twin hearts will be here to stay

But they've never seen the immovable float away

This island that stands in our way

Will be the one on which we'll stay

Create a home where our hearts will be gay

Never again to stray

They say we'll never be one

But they've never seen this unbreakable bond

They say we'll never be beside or around

Even though the best in us is bound

Closer than our feet to the ground

They say we'll never be safe

In each other's embrace

But they've never seen the impossible made possible

They say you'll never lift me up

From this dark hopeless pit

That the murky waters that hold me down

Will always be my swampy ground

They've never known you like I do

And they've never seen one as powerful as you

They say I'll drown in this endless sea

That you'll never swim to rescue me

If only they knew the strength of your limbs

Or the power your lungs bring

They would only say that the angry waters

Would instead guide our ship to eternity sail

WE'LL RIDE

When this search for a hill of gold gets dreary

And our stubborn hearts get old and weary

We'll scale rigid mountains holding on but barely

Our deep mutual connection grounds us dearly

Friendships may come and like the wind they swiftly go

Empty spaces left that dims our glow

But yours satiate the gaps in my soul

Warming every chamber chasing away the snow

I count you among the rare and precious few

Who'll start fireworks amidst the midnight dew

Understanding my demons and my angels too

Riding high on bursts of clouds every day anew

You uncaged my thrill over waters it set sail

I surge with life even when my dry bones are frail

Epic adrenaline presses against my ungroomed brain

My imprisoned heart just escaped without bail

I pray this boiling energy never cools

I'll wear these scars like a bedrock that on me pool

The ripples electrify yet snips my pride

On life's rolling waves together, we'll ride

JOURNEY TO LOVE

As I sail the seas on this roller coaster ride

Wishing for you to be by my side

I pray that my God will be my guiding light

Illuminating my path into the pitch-dark, night

They say preparation is the key

That opens the heart of you and me

But in desperate and needy times

I seem to falter when I should be prime

I search for the one who'll fit this mold

Becoming love that will never grow old

A strong magnetic field that pulls and grows

Activating a heart that's asleep and cold

When you and I finally become one

A wholeness that we'll both understand

Complimenting every chamber of our hearts

A glue that will never pull apart

When the band ceases to play

And the stars close their eyes

Untie the tangled thread that binds

So our tired souls can fly

ENOUGH

The infinite supply of gold dust

Laced in between the earth's crust

Or endless layers of pearls

Beneath the ocean's floor

If for one moment I could compare

Though their value to many seems rare

Still it's not enough

Of all the stars in the night skies

And the full moon shining bright

If I could gather all the raindrops

Or steal the flowering plants and crops

My abundant coffers will overflow with food

And from my body cheerfulness will exude

Still it won't be enough

There's a dream that's getting louder

Amidst the echos of a world of noise

The heart's songs play in whispers

To the orchestra of fear

But though thousands of others pursue

And their offers are brand new

Still it won't be enough if it's not with you

A PIECE OF ME

Today our eyes may not meet

You're far away and I miss seeing your smile

But though distance separates you and I

I hope you know that I'll always keep you close

Today our cheeks may not touch

And it will hurt my heart just as much

But your presence transcends all physicality

I hope you know that you're the wind beneath my wings

Today you go to your special place

Enjoy every moment build memories and slow your pace

I'll be here when you get home my dear

I hope you take a piece of me with you

I CAN'T WAIT

I can't wait to hold your hands

On a stroll in a distant land

And bask in the newness of love

Where the focus is just us

I can't wait to love you forever

Loudly but as sweet as the silence

Kiss your face and feel your warm embrace

Under the reflection of your starry gaze

I can't wait to bear our children

For they will have your smile

And possess your elegant style

With unique designs and intellectual flair

I can't wait to wake up beside you

Morning after morning until eternity

Then watch you fall asleep

Then I'll be complete

Missing Heart

If one petal should fall

Every time I long to hear you call

There would be no flowers for the bees

So fruit and honey would follow in the dinosaurs thrall

If one star should go dim

Whenever I miss feeling you skin to skin

Then the skies would weep to the melody of a funeral hymn

And seek the peaceful tree to sit on its lowest limb

If my heartbeat would only slow

With the memories of the secrets that only us lovers know

Then on the branch of the peaceful tree that hangs most low

I would sit with my memories all aglow

If the distant star upon which I wish

Would only bring me your love and happiness

And cease to give me cheerful promises

Then my spirit would be buoyed and I would live in bliss

MORNINGS LIKE THIS

On mornings like this when I awake on an icy hill

Though the fireplace is lit the cold lingers still

The embrace of my love awaits across the distant sea

But today I awake to face the memories of you and me

On mornings like this my heart is in a lonely place

Knowing that this emptiness that stares me in the face

Though temporary will crush my pride beneath its feet

While I await the moment when our bodies will finally meet

Though mornings like these are feared and rare

They fuel my heart's engine and shifts it to the highest gear

Calls my blood to once dead organs that were bare

And gives me hope for my grand return to your breast my dear

On mornings like this when I wake up all alone

In a huge king-sized bed just lying there on my own

Knowing that for breakfast I will have leftovers that are as dry as
bone

I am grateful to be alive but my heart gives a silent groan

My old heart ails from breaking and constant heartburn

As my bigger head spin tales of you and your grand return

Tales that my gut knows are cremated ashes of a love now fit for an
urn

My awakening brings little joys but rather great concern

But on mornings like this when the painful moments slowly crawl
away

I will be gentle with myself and take a moment to pray

To the God of my forefathers for him to make a way

For me to from this sad and lonely morning make myself a better day

My better day will come when instead of a memory

Of my flawed and broken construct of our history

I will have you here in actuality

Lying in my big and lonely bed awaking next to me

YOU ARE

For every moment that I drift

Especially those when you kiss my lips

I've entered a mystical realm

Filled with love-stricken spells

And continuous incantations that won't quell

I feel as though I'm weak

Laying helplessly in defeat

Cause bliss shape shift and retreats

When I'm ready to climb the lover's peak

And my reality runs towards me full speed

But then you tighten your embrace

And every fear is erased

Every insecurity gone without a trace

My heart rhythm takes on a different pace

And butterflies celebrate deep within my inner space

You are the reason

For every fire that's lit in my imperfect heart.

For every great journey that I'll ever start.

For every attempt to be successful and smart.

And I hope one day we'll cease being apart.

Missing You

I'll never be able to say the right words

The ones that express my feelings out loud

My stomach will knot my throat in a chokehold

That's because I miss you my world is crippled and cold

I miss you when the sun is low in the sky

The light disappears and my hope starts to die

Pandora's box cracks open again

And the darkness begins to overwhelm the light

I miss you when the blossoms begin to bloom

These flowers now grow from the dirt of my gloom

Watered by my sea of tears and winter's monsoon

Oh how I long for the peace of high noon

I miss you as the clock ticks away

For the time that we lose will not return one day

I'll whisper a prayer and hope it comes your way

Until then I still miss you today

My Ride or Die

Sit with me in my cozy nest

Draw close to me as I rest

I won't ever protest

If I begin to salivate and get wet

Throw your arms across my chest

Allow me to get lost in your caress

You'll find that every part of my interest

Lies within your world of brokenness

I want to lower my disguise

So you too can get lost in my eyes

For within it is a world where there are no lies

And my open heart you will never despise

You are the bridge over my stormy way

Turning my roadblocks into roadways

And though you appear to never stay

I desire to follow even if led astray

I WISH

I wish you were a listening ear

Especially on days I need you here

Or when life diminishes my will to spare

The very thing that makes you seem near

I wish you could be the gentle wind

Softly massaging my love thirst skin

So that when I am advanced in years

It will sing loudly a youthful hymn

I wish you were my invisible cocoon

With no intention to release me at my high noon

So that when time removes its sheltering hand

My fearsome self-confidence will be left to stand

I wish I could summon you to my side

Even when the season is not Yuletide

For when my heart and head collide

Your love is all I need to survive the darkest tide

LOVE

It hurts

It's demanding

It's expensive

It's selfish

It's jealous

But when it's reciprocal

It's overwhelming

And nonsensical

We all crave this strange brew

Yet some often run away without a clue

When the butterflies nest deep within like glue

Bitter pills are easier to chew

It possesses the same meaning to few

But some will play with it and dispose the best they knew

Then repercussions knock them out of their shoes

And they lose the thing that makes the best stew

It requires an openness that's agitating

And a transparency that's unsettling

But when two hearts choose unity

The chances are higher for impunity

So when past battles they must conjure

Together they'll be enough to endure

To weather storms till the sunshine is restored

And be in love forevermore

CHAPTER
The Discovery

There were a few people who had stayed the journey with me and were special to me. Lisa (Jer) was one of them. That same girl I met that first day of college almost four years prior was a force to be reckoned with. Life wasn't always easy for either of us, but she identified with the struggles, and often reassured me that it shall pass. The sleep overs at her house, and the nights out partying were experience I needed and Jer was there to keep me grounded as she was a few years older and way more experienced in the street. Lisa was a girl on a mission to win at any cost. Her drive to succeed and create for herself a career that she could live off for years to come, was one of the reasons I became close with her. She had started at the community college level and by this time, had entered the undergraduate program. Although we kept in touch all the time, seeing her at college again my second time around was something we both welcomed. I had transferred some credits from the previous course so I only needed to complete one year to receive my teacher education certification. The students in my group were all professionals, some of whom had already been teaching for a number of years, or aspired to switch professions. In order to satisfy the curriculum, a three month's internship at a high school or college was required. There were a lot of "hands on" work and although not my first choice, I applied myself sufficiently to receive another "Honors" at graduation.

My "prince charming" would visit me very regularly especially on weekends. We would spend the weekends together at my place and visit his mother in between days. The first time he introduced me to his mother was most memorable as I never really had a good "mother-in-law" relationship before. Mama as she was affectionately called was a 5'3" powerhouse of a woman. Although she was well into her 70's, she never let her age prevented her from running her house. That memorable night, she sat in her kitchen grating cassava to prepare "bammy" for her sister-in-law who was visiting. "Mama this is Jan; Jane meet my mother" he said in passing. She looked up from her grater and glanced at me briefly, or so I thought. "Hi Jan" she said and quickly continued with her chore. He picked up what he went for and we said our good byes and left. Confused by my brief encounter, I wondered whether or not I made a good first impression. We didn't speak about it again but he continued to take me there on the weekend visits. I grew on my new mother-in-law, and before long we were like peas in a pod. One day she confided in me that she didn't like me at first because she thought that I looked too young for her son. He was 30 and the time and I was 10 years his junior.

Time flies so quickly when you're having fun they say. This particular weekend, he said he wouldn't be able to come see me and I was crushed. I waited the entire week to be refueled and he didn't show.

I Can Fly

If healing wasn't the ultimate thing

And my open wounds wouldn't flail in the wind

For all to see that I'm surrendering

To the circumstances that loneliness brings

But though I have one broken wing

And my heart refuses to sing

When our brokenness together clings

I can fly

My life was once full of color

Of dreams and unimaginable valor

I've had ancestors in my ear when my thoughts get shallow

So the path I walk will not devour

The darkness sometimes creeps in through the light

And the daytime turns into night

But in the midst of my unimaginable plight

Your embrace is my delight

And I can fly

When the greenery of summer turns to fall

I'll miss the sun and the sweet sound of the bird's call

And as the summer disappears

It takes with it my heartfelt cheer

But if I awake to the morning's autumn hues

And the cool breeze push away the blues

I'll dare to step onto the grass all wet with dew

For I am at home in your embrace

And then I'll fly

Deflated, I decided to call him. The phone went to voicemail as it often does. I had his house phone number but had never used it, so I decided to call it. Shock turned to anger when the recording on the voicemail was a woman's voice. I called again just to make sure I heard right – I did hear right. I went to my sister and asked her to call the number because I needed a second opinion or confirmation, and sure enough, a woman's voice – "we're not here to take your call at this time. Please leave a message and we'll return your call." What does she mean by "we?" I shouted. "Who the @#&* is that"? My sister tried to calm me "maybe that's his friend. Some people used other people's voice on their voicemail." She suggested. She said "WE!" I responded with eyes popping out of my head and flailing hands. I stormed to my room and buried my head in my pillow so they wouldn't hear my screams of pain. How could I not see the red flags? Is there a "we" that I didn't know about? Was this too good to be true so I ignored everything else? Why didn't I question this before nor do my investigation before I'm so heavily entwined in this? My mind was overloaded with questions that I couldn't answer. I dialed the cell phone number all night and each time the same automated voice. Afraid to dial the house phone, lest she answers this time, I decided to write down my thoughts so I could let him know exactly how I felt in the moment. Tragedy brought out something in me that I had never even thought was there. I searched for a scratch pad and found one that had a gun logo that appeared to be from the Wild West.

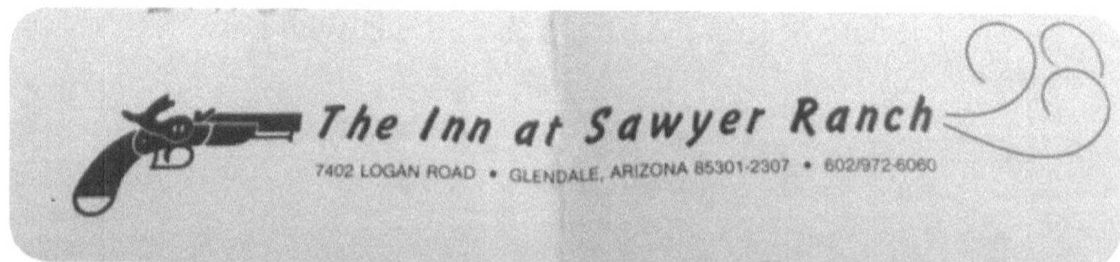

I had no idea where I got it because I had never been to "The Inn at Sawyer Ranch in Glendale, Arizona. Page 289 of that scratchpad chronicled my response- and I wrote:

I HAVE TO GO

I lay down at nights, my pillow wet with tears that tell the tale of hurt beyond what words can describe

I know I have to go

I love him so much – I can't stand the thought of him lying beside another woman

I have to go because I don't understand why it hurts so much

I cry because I feel less than a "princess" to him

He will never leave her – she was first

I have to go because I can't live life knowing that the man, I love is loving another

I know I won't be happy for a while, but I'm a strong woman and I will get by… eventually

I can't get him out of my mind, but I have to go

I am so complete with him. How do I turn my back on my happiness?

How do I say goodbye to my heartbeat? But I MUST GO!

I have to go before my heart is completely committed to him – but… how far am I from that?

I've already slipped deeply in love with him and I don't know how to stop myself.

*I need him – she needs him – she lives with him – I am all alone… …
OH GOD HELP ME TO LET GO!*

I'm so happy with him by my side, yet so sad away from him.

I miss him – I need him. Help me make the right decision baby… LET ME GO! STOP ME BEFORE I FALL TOO DEEP, before you have to watch me turn into an unhappy hopeless CASE! No… don't stop me now.

I love you sweetheart – I always will

But….I MUST GO!

NO MORE FIGHT

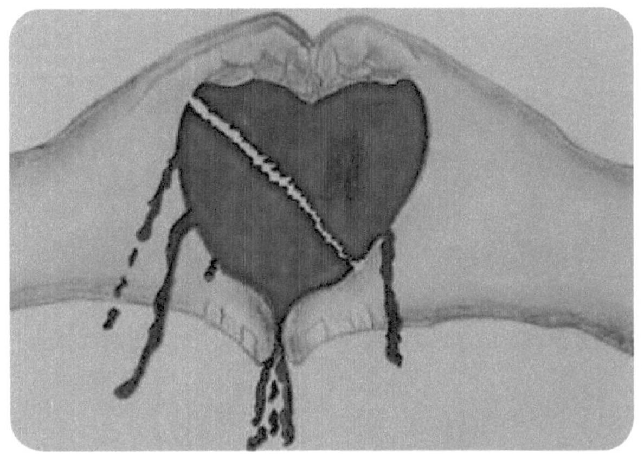

Today my broken spirit speaks

Of battlefield stories and regrets

Waiting for daybreak alarms to sound

Since it lived to fight and be found

I sit naked and motionless in my sea of tears

Living in limbo of uncertainties and fears

Praying that my Almighty father hears

As my drowning whispers fill the air

This lonely road is filled with twists and turns

Scraping against my listless bones

A martyr to all the things untold

Fraying the edges of a heart that's old and cold

I keep knocking at the door of fate

Searching for the righteous route of escape

Begging my captors to pry open the gates

Or release these chains causing me headaches

Now I stare at a future of broken dreams

Where life's a fight for everything it seems

Building an empty princess's palace

Paying for happiness that was always free

The weekend came, and sure enough, he showed up. I couldn't bring myself to resist him. For a moment I forgot all about my hurt and pain the moment I saw that Nissan coming through my gate. I'm usually quiet when I'm most upset because I don't want to say things I will regret. My body fought with my heart and my head. Emotions overwhelmed me. My body yearned for his embrace, my heart hurt by his betrayal, and my stubborn head told me that I MUST GO! How do I resolve this situation so that I satisfy them all? Who wins, the heart, head, or body? I watched him take his usual stride towards the house and my head's protest slowly drifted into the background. My body relaxed at his embrace, but my head continued to protest. The heartache grew less and before I knew it, we were one.

My Weak Mind

There was a time when I loved you

You use to tickle me and I would laugh so hard

My eyes would weld up with happy tears

My belly would tighten with breath stopping bursts

And at times I would bend over and clap for fear

That my lungs couldn't handle my excitement and glee

There was a time when the sun always came out

The trees swayed to the beat of the gentle wind

The birds sang with me a tune I understood

My eyes were a beautiful brown globe and I could see possibilities

My loins held the power of my Nubian genes and I loved every inch
of it

But I taught you to have a weak mind

When did I stop loving you?

How did I stop fighting for you?

Why did I push the sun away?

Where did my poise and pride lay?

The person starring back at me is a stranger

Have I taught me to have a weak mind?

I must find myself

Push away those clouds and see the light again

Train my mind to slow down and smell the morning dew

Ignore all the thoughts that said I will never be new

Put on that pretty dress and enjoy the stride and those breathtaking
views

I must untrain my weak mind

The confusion of my emotions triggered a river of tears. I couldn't
express how I felt because it was literally everything at the same
time – love, pain, indifference, empathy, sympathy (for myself), and
everything in between. How did I get to this place? I promised my ten
year old self that I would never be caught in this situation, but – here
I am. I resorted to my best friend – my notepad. In the midst of my
confusion and sobbing I wrote…….

I didn't expect this from him. I thought he was different from other
men. I thought all my hurt was over that day I fell in love with him
and I would be the happiest woman in the world. Why couldn't he just
be honest with me and let me decide on whether or not I wanted to be
with him? He deceived me and I will never forgive him. I feel like I

will never find happiness – a relationship that is picture perfect. I prefer to be alone than to know I have to share him – with someone he had before me. I can't stand the thought of him sleeping with someone else, living with someone else, loving "princess!" I see no future for "us" although he tries to convince me otherwise. I will never accept her and that is why I'm not going to stay. He will never leave her so I will go. I LOVE HIM – but this is the only way now. I am so disappointed that he killed my dreams – at least so soon.

I'm hurting so bad right now I can't even begin to explain its depth. I have never felt this kind of hurt before, even though I claim to have love and lost. I told you it was better to end the relationship, but now I wonder what hurts more – sharing you or losing you. I don't want to share you, but I won't lose you. I LOVE YOU SO MUCH and I don't know why! I wish I could just cut out this part of my life and continue with the life we had. I DON'T WANT TO LOSE YOU! (Please help me Lord, don't let him shut me out of his life because if he does, my life would not be the same.) I don't want to learn to live without you because that would be impossible. I still want to spend 99 years with you sweetheart, and have your children. I don't care if another woman loves you because I know she cannot love you as much as I do. But I envy her! I envy her because of the trust you feel towards her, the confidence that I think she feels when she's with you – one that you don't have for me. I'm sorry if I hurt you. I need you and I can't live without you. I want you to teach me the virtues of life and the path to the perfect relationship – one that I crave so badly now. I guess hurt is a normal part of the game. I saw my mother live a life I didn't want to repeat. Sweetheart, promise me I can count on you for a life far from misery. I want to be the only one in your life. Please let me know if it's too late to start over. I think I deserve another chance not to make the same mistake again, but to make it right. I LOVE YOU BABY! I don't want to lose you – not now – not ever. I don't know if I can convince you that I need you this much, but whatever you do, remember I will always love you. If I knew then what I know now, I would have saved forever for you. I want you to save you for me.

I LOVE YOU BABY – ALWAYS

BLEEDING HEART

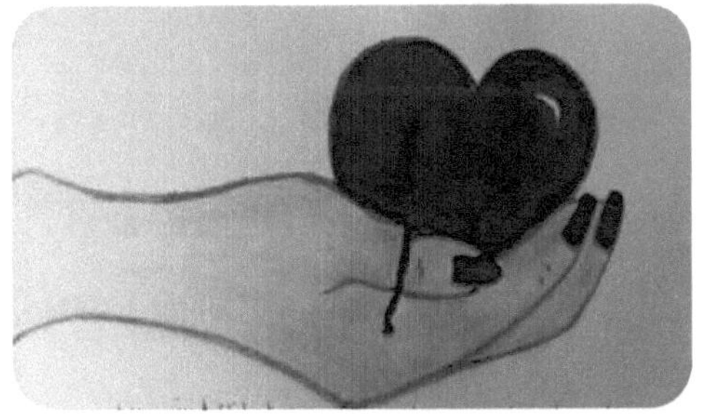

I gave you my heart… all of it!

That was not my intention but you had me at first sight

Every day I wonder why

That view from across the room was so captivating

And your energy was so exhilarating

Now my soul is tied to this tri…angular vine

The required parts that make the whole

Breaks my pride and bends me at an angle

Yet it feeds my attention wow don't let me forget to mention

The TLC that's given and just enough divided into fractions

To allow the heart to grow fonder discrediting any distractions

This tri…..angular vine is hooked deep in my being

Daily I drink from a wishing well

No one else can my secrets tell

They say stolen waters are sweet

But it burns the belly the after effect is surely not neat

Causing me to introspect but in retrospect

This tri…..angular vine satisfies my soul

I gave you my heart… all of it!

You held it so tightly it learned to breathe your air

Walk lightly my dear because I fear

That my bleeding heart will get scared

Cease to exist and other parts get smeared

But I'll listen to its language so I'll find my next gear

For this tri…..angular affair I should beware

SAD RAIN

When the rain tap dances on my rooftop

And I'm thinking of the way you lit my heart's fire

Or the sound of your footsteps massaging my desires

It reminds me of the day you walked into my life

The rain is the background slow jam as I melt into embrace

The Shaman beats that set my heart at ease

And as they drip bit by bit slowly

I am reminded of special moments

Today as it's torrential waters flow

It washed away the memories I hold

My weeping pines bowed low

And exposed a side that I've never known

Oh rain my trust in you is now lost

You promised roses from the seeds I tossed

These thorns have lined the walls I must cross

And you trample on my blood soaked heart

I felt the caress of your melancholy drops

I loved the sweetness of your musical sound

What should I expect from you today?

Or do you like to see me sad?

Time stood still for a couple of days. My auto pilot kicked in and my muscle memory saved the day. He didn't answer my calls, neither did he return them. Again I turned to my best friend…..

The Things I Miss Most

Firstly, I miss your presence always.

I know that I can't have you around all day, but why can't I have you
all night?

Where are you when a woman needs you?

Pins and needles beneath my feet trying to figure out what I did to
deserve this.

Secondly, I miss your touch.

It makes me feel all woman, yet it's so rare.

I treasure the moments that we share – only heaven knows such bliss.

Thirdly, your warmth overwhelms me – fuel for my bones.

I see it in your eyes - I feel it in your embrace

The way you speak makes me tingle with glee

It is just too good to be true (I hope you notice my vivacity when
you're with me)

Fourthly, and most of all, I MISS YOU! – ALL OF YOU!

I cannot find the most appropriate medium to express it, but I tried the
ways I know how. I would love to have and to hold, in sickness and in
health, for better or worst until death do us part.

I have found in you the power to connect on a level that most humans
can't, and I really MISS YOU!

Christmas came and went, but the lonely nights continued to press hard against my chest. The weekend visits remained constant and although I longed for him to give himself completely, I inadvertently settled for what I could have. I hoped for the New Year to find "us" together – at least a "chups" at midnight. 10 o'clock came and went. I feared 11pm but it was inevitable. My heart began to grow heavier as the clock ticked on past midnight. 1999 said its goodbyes and 2000 found me alone. Tears flowed like a river and my notepad beckoned.

What did I do to deserve this?

He was not beside me to say happy New Year!

He was not here to kiss me under the mistletoe and now no kiss after midnight.

Instead, he was in his Princess' arms.

I wanted to be the last to make love to him for 1999 and the first to see him in 2000.

What did I do to deserve this?

Is something wrong with me?

Lord, please send me someone who will love me enough to not want to be with another woman. I am tired of being alone at nights thinking about someone who don't want me to be his only Princess.

He says he loves me, but why does his love hurt so much?

I refuse to stay hurting like this!

I need to be happy!

I need to feel loved through action and not just words!

I need to feel wanted!

Why me Lord?

Please answer my prayers Lord

The dawn of day two of 2000 felt like I was driving on punctured tires – rim on road! How did I find myself in this position? My reality played like a broken record in my head. Tears streamed down my face and my only friend I could tell my problems waits. It brought me solace every time and kept my secrets safe. I wrote because I couldn't break the news to others, that the love of my life loved another. I couldn't get off the roller coaster although it passed several stations – some very attractive ones. I was trapped and it felt like my destiny.

You painted the most beautiful picture of life……one that I have never before seen.

No one has ever managed to do that.

You are the perfect man I hoped for – a scarce commodity only for a few.

But alas! I wonder – how could such beauty go unseen?

How could I have thought you were single, celibate of free?

I thought myself lucky – maybe my dreams came through.

Then it did – at least for a short while! Now, I don't know.

Save me from a nightmare – please wake me up!

The truth came out!

He has his princess!

I was stopped in my tracks.

Should I forgive and forget?

How will I get over this?

I was just beginning to enjoy my forever when yesterday snatched it away.

Disappointed – hurt – betrayed, and everything else in between.

I know he loves me – but he loves her too.

What do I do?

What can I do?

I can't live with this!

But I must!

I won't accept it!

But how do I live without my heart?

I wish I could forget him.

I am sorry we met because I wouldn't have experienced the depth of what my heart could feel. Then it wouldn't hurt so much. But if a heart can love another like this – why not my heart?

I float in colorful roses on a cloud when I'm with you.

Moments, though rare, are the epitome of my existence.

I never want to forget him – only because I don't know how!

He was as good at consoling me as he was at hurting me. I felt overwhelming compassion for him after the hurt passed and nothing else mattered when I lay in his arms.

I don't understand – but I think its love!

I'm feeling things I cannot explain

Why do I miss him so much?

I was not ready to let go. Could there be an endless weekend?

I wished there were two of him – one for work and one for me.

I'm not ashamed to admit it.

You are my only spark and I'm really cold without you.

With you I have everything – I feel complete!

Eternity is what I aim for with you.

His usual weekend visit didn't happen until Sunday afternoon. He came in a different car that appear to be a rental. He left "stuff" with me since he had things to do. So I looked at his "stuff." Just when I thought my heart couldn't take another blow – here comes an uppercut! A love letter from his New York Lover!

The blood drained from my body and my mind refused to think. The noise of my surroundings was drowned by my moans. My organs crashed into each other as I hugged my oversized pillow in an effort to stabilize them. Why me Lord!? I looked at my notepad and it too turned on me. No one to turn to – no comfort. The throbbing of my head reminded me that I should find an avenue or else my body may shut down to save itself. No one could ever hurt me like this. No one will ever do it again! As I sat on the edge of my bed, I looked around to see if there was anything else that may reveal more about my love. I stayed locked in my room just enough time to compose myself. He said that he was coming back, but I never knew where he went. He forgot that his "love" letter was among his stuff. "What is it baby?" The familiar voice prompted me to open my eyes. My tears gave me away. I couldn't explain in as many words so I pointed to his "love letter." "You read my letter?" His eyes bulged and his voice deepened. I got angrier. I couldn't believe his reaction. He slammed the door and and left. I retreated to my safe haven. Everything caved in on me that night – walls, body and head. I felt like I had no tears left and I wouldn't be able to withstand the pain. I thought about walking but it had already gotten dark. How will I make it through the night? I dragged myself up, put on a pair of jeans and a hooded sweater and went to the kitchen for a knife. I had a small carving knife that could fit inconspicuously in my pocket. I headed out to search for my sanity. My head was winning the race against my feet. I didn't know what I was thinking about because my head kept switching channels. Am I going crazy? I kept walking. Head upright, hands in pocket, no destination in mind, no sounds heard and no one seen. The cool of the night must have massaged my brain to consciousness because I started noticing lights and people and vehicles. It suddenly dawned on me that I was passing through the town. I had walked a few miles and it is now well past midnight. I need to go back! How do I face the memories/loneliness of my room? The gloom awaited me and I feared it greatly. Should I continue walking until daylight? That way I won't have to face my dying heart. I began to feel tired – physically and mentally. I better head back. The walk was slow. I glanced at my phone to see the time. 1 am gazed back at me. Predators lurked at this time of the night, but they may have seen the fearlessness in my stride, so they didn't come close. As I turned on to home stretch and through my room door. I felt enough energy to talk to my best friend – my notepad:

OH NIGHT

Loathsome desires dance in my head

Craving for joy to take me to bed

I beg my God to make me empty

For the night showers burdens that's plenty

Laughter frowns at my pain

No sense trying cause it would be in vain

Not even a glimmer of light there's only rain

This darkness hugs my soul oh what disdain

Oh how I wish we could be like old friends

Past merry times were all well spent

Our meetings use to turn on the sparkle in my eyes

Now I fear the wrath of your jealous contempt

Joy seems to have deserted this place

For greener pastures it left in a haste

You linger longer than I could ever imagine

And light refused to push you away

I begged for peace to release me

But your dominant hand seduced her soul

She stares at my gloom from a distance

For Peace didn't know your secrets to tell

Oh night I beg of you to quell

This inferno that dug a hole as deep as hell

Call a cease fire on your dark angels

I long for us to be bosom friends again

APOLOGY

I don't ask for much.

I didn't see this coming but I survived you.

My self-inflicted pain reminds me that I'm human and I err.

I'm sorry self.

I apologize heart.

I failed you body.

I'm terribly sorry 10-year-old self.

Forgive me for being careless, blind and in love

Forgive me for not protecting you from the inevitable.

It was just too good to be true!

Now we have to regroup and move on!

We have to agree on a strategy!

Head says go!

Body says go!

Heart says NO!

Back to square one!

How do I share him with Princess and D?

What a fight! Who wins?

Only time will tell.

The memories of our beach rendezvous flashed violently in my head, and I so wanted to be near her so she could massage my weary brain.

THE THERAPIST

Sand and me are a shrewd pair

Because we both desire to be near

Waters blue incandescent hue

Nature's therapy is all we knew

I see the sun peep through

Pushing away the deep-sea blues

Pitching a light just as bright

A spark that's enough to scare my fright

The rough waves crash against my feet

A skilled masseuse a sensuous waltz

My blood responds and warms my thighs

A recharge only from the one on high

She disappears behind an ageless sunset

Her peerless beauty left behind

Passing the baton to the magical night

Dropping its blanket all to my delight

Alternatives have been pushed aside

Because heaven bowed to kiss my thighs

Handpicked me to be it's client

Nature's therapy I can't deny

LONG ROAD TO NOWHERE

There is a road filled with pain and suffering

Smooth at first glance but treachery lies ahead

The lush greenery beyond its golden gates

And a captivating backdrop beyond imagination

On that lonely road to nowhere

They say misery loves company

But I would've taken misery if only with you

Though the sun's rays are brighter

Its heat burns like a torch against my skull

On that lonely road to nowhere

For years a slave to the beat of my heart

With hopes of shades along its path

Raining shelterless eyes for no one else

Lured with the bait of promises but

Only dashed dreams lay along that lonely road to nowhere

Someone should have told me

Someone should have showed me

Oh if only someone who walked this road before

Mom I wished I had listened to the tales

Of that lonely road to nowhere

No families live along that road

No plans survive on that road

No health issues resolved on that road

No peace of mind on that road

If only I could get off that lonely road to nowhere

Members only signs everywhere

Sign up specials not very rare

Models few and far in between

Cause there's no one to hear the cries and the screams

If only I could find the reverse gear on that lonely road to nowhere

The measure of a man is in his dash

Where's, what's, how's, and who's

Good, bad, happy, sad

But pain beyond flesh is undeserved

Even on this long lonely road to nowhere

So I will scream it all over the hilltops and paint it all over the plains

Unplug my heart's GPS and take a shot at freedom street

And if I die from the wounds in this survival game

Label my headstone "scared by that lonely road to nowhere"!

Cloud Angel

You had me at hello

You had the ability to lift me up higher than anyone could

And only you could knock the wind from under my sails

When you were good you were great

When you were bad my heart would break

My soul danced to the beat of your rhythm

Every move every turn all your isms

High on a cloud I would shine like a prism

Radiating love light created only by your mannerisms

The fall from atop that cloud was steep

Heartbreak misery and confusion was mine to reap

If only in my heart you could peep

A little compassion would give me a creep

Why did you come into my life?

I was hoping one day to be your wife

On some days there were gut wrenching jabs just like a knife

On other days my heart would melt with nothing but nice

If only you could be my cloud angel.

DANCE IN THE RAIN

I wish I could find that perfect spot

One where few life forces exist and some not

Only tulips among greenery and trees

Flowers blooming amid the crisp winter breeze

When its warmth hits the atmosphere

I wish I could dance in the rain

My naked soul I would reveal

When the beauty of sunrise appears

Awakening my dormant musical chair

From whispering chants to loud sounding cheers

Plucking my every string without fear

Then I would have found a brand-new gear

When enchanting fragrances draw near

Tickling the radiant atmosphere

Parading through my external spaces

But if the arid cloud would break free

And let its golden showers drain

At last, I'll dance in the rain

Hurricane

I get lost in the infinity of those eyes

My head warns me but all my heart wants is

To love you even though I can't have you

I just desire to be your everything

And I won't ask for anything except all of you

The phone rings on end and I'm trying to make amends

though it's not me who should try to defend your actions

Your voice sounds so good on the recording

I wished my ear was up against those lips

When the shivers make their way down my length to my hips

But I'm caught up in your spiral and I'm falling deep

Where do you go late at nights

What do you do without me by your side

How do you feel when you see me cry

Why do you take me on this roller coaster ride

When my love for you I cannot deny

I'm drowning in the sea of your deceit

Feeling helplessly cold recognizing my defeat

I never signed up just to repeat

My sentiments of pity that messes with all of me

Do you know that I still wait just to see you?

I need a shield from the rain

Wishing I would feel you like a gentle wind massaging my under
belly

flowing beneath my wings

Toss me around only when we dance to sounds from our heart's
strings

Hold me close when I need refueling in my limbs

You're a Hurricane sweetheart and I want to feel your sting

LOVE WHISPERS

When hate is blaring in the wind

And greed's brazen hand is busy still

For all the hurt that tightly cling

Love sings sweet melodies with its soft whisperings

A rigid shell I was today

Bombarded by fear and dismay

My feet refused to be on their way

To love disguised as one who'll stay

In life's dark and starless nights

When my lonely heart wants to fight

I hear a soft tremulous voice

Reminding me that in patience I'll find delight

Today I'll throw caution to the wind

For you have been a constant thrill

Though challenges mount we continue to build

And love's loud whispers linger still

I read my journal "posts" over and over. I couldn't believe that I was already finding a way to justify his actions. The tears couldn't stop flowing and I didn't know how to get past the hurt, or leave him. I'm upset with him, upset with Princess, upset with D, but most of all I was mad at me. Now I not only find myself in a love triangle, it has officially become a rectangle. Who else am I up against? Will I discover more if I stay? That thought drove away any sleep that could possibly enter my being, and before I could wink, the sun was peeping through my window. I continued to pen my thoughts:

I cried

I cried the tears of a woman who lost her child

I cried the tears of a woman who is unable to conceive

I cried the tears of the woman yearning for a stable emotional life

I cried because I loved

I cried tears because he left for another woman's bed

I cried the tears of a woman wishing for a companion who will never make her lonely

I cried only because I loved

How much longer will I cry?

Will my tears run dry or will they pour like rain?

I cried because I felt pain that no illness could bring

I cried because I felt "love" suffering

I cried only because I love you!

Days turned into a week, and my weekend came and went and he continued to stay away. No phone calls, no text messages, no visits. His princess had blocked my number so I didn't try calling him although my heart burned like a thin film of paper. I tried so hard to forget him but my heart wouldn't let me. Every night my pillow served as my basin to catch my tears. I watched the sun chase away the moon, and I prayed for my sanity. I wrote myself an affirmation:

I will get over you

I will learn to live without you

I will distance myself from you so that you will never be able to reach me.

No one will affect me this way again

Only I can hurt me now – and I won't!

Week two came and went. It didn't get any better. I wore my best self every day and broke down like a puzzle at nights. The late night strolls kept me energized and I know that I had to stop myself from dying …...Slowly. But hc kept walking all over my mind.

One Master

How can you serve two masters at the same time?

What are you trying to prove?

Is it possible to "love" more than one person, and keep them both happy?

Are you a Solomon with 300 wives and 700 concubines?

Remember, only the fittest will survive!

One day you will face the music and I don't know if you will dance.

When will you narrow your choice to one?

I will come to the wedding.

I want to see your child.

I want to tell him that I love his dad.

I want to go on……but how?

The familiar sound of that Nissan stanza filled the air, and my stomach began to knot. It has been two weeks and I wasn't sure what he wanted. He pulled into the driveway and parked for a few minutes. I starred through my bedroom window, unsure of how to react. I watched the door open and then I got up to open the grill gate. He held me really closely and whispered "I missed you." I didn't know that I had tears until I heard him speak. I melted into his arms and my dam broke letting through a flood of tears. His lips searched and caressed my face. The kisses were gentle. My knees gave way and I knew there was no turning back. The orchestra played the most beautiful song I have ever heard……but it was all in my head. He paused just long enough to lead me to my room. There were tiny lights in the ceiling that made the dark the most beautiful scene I've ever witnessed…. the birds cooed and chirped amidst the husky whispers of sweet nonsense. Our mixed sweat tasted sweet. My gravity defying body came to its senses as we fall into each other's arms… that was when I realized that there were no special effects in the room…..it was all in my head! Reality hit like a ton of bricks and the tears flowed once more. I attempted to speak, but the sound wouldn't come out. He hugged me so close, I almost felt suffocated. Confusion set in……how does one love so hard and hurt so equally? Familiar feelings crept into my being. Anger pushed her way to the surface and as I attempted to pull away from his embrace, he clutched me even tighter. The strength of his arms was no match for my anger. Attempts to hold me failed so he propped himself against my headboard and waited for the storm to be over. His bulging eyes appeared to be jealous and welded with tears as he starred at me. I tried to decipher the war between my head, body and heart. "I hate to see you cry" he said in a cracked tone. He stretched out his hands to bring me close to him but my back was glued against the wall as I brushed him off. It appeared as if my head was winning. The protest kept going and my poor heart cried a river. He flung his head back amidst a deep sigh as if he gave up trying to console me. With abated breath he blurted "I LOVE YOU!" That was all I needed to hear. As if a code was entered, my hands opened, my back unglued from the wall, and my body began to move towards his. Nothing else mattered now. Although I had heard those words so many times before, this time it was the one thing that unlocked every chamber of my being. Round two was on…

I adjusted my eyes to the glimpse of light peeping through my curtains. It was daylight but I didn't want to move. The steady beat of his heart calmed my mind as I thought about a picture I saw a while back. Lush green grass covered the flat rocks that led to the water. It appeared as if the mountains positioned themselves to perfectly contain a section of the sea. The angle from which the picture was taken showed the reflection of the mountains in the water all around, and it looked like two palms. Between the two mountains stood smaller peaks with the sky perfectly outlined in the backdrop. The foot of the mountain towards the section that was submerged into the water appeared rough and the top a little smoother. There was no movement in the water. The unnerving stillness of the water triggered thought of danger in the deep. How could the water be so still but the mountains told a tale of destruction? This beautiful scene held sad hidden stories. One of security and insecurity, beauty and ugliness, freedom and bondage, love and hate, dependence and independence, strength and courage, culpability and embarrassment, pride and prowess….and everything in between. And I was one with this scene. Oh how I wished I was one of those clouds in the backdrop. Free to go in any direction without being cornered by mountains that holds on despite being constantly scraped. My disappointment was not enough to keep me from responding favorable to his lips on my forehead. My mind came back to my here and now and my fears disappeared as he smiled at me. I woke up in his arms and my heart was dancing excitedly in my chest……at least for that moment. But it was time for him to leave. I knew what I was up against. Why did I not stop myself? I couldn't be mad at him… this time I blamed me.

BETRAYAL

Oh heart, why did you make a mockery of me?

Oh body, why do you tingle at every thought of him?

Pussy, why do you continue to betray me?

Head, why do you refuse to stand up for me?

When will you realize that the roller coaster goes around in a circle?

How do you plan to resolve this mess?

He has to go home to his princess….and you are just his release!

Now what?

You got one night…..one night of lies and deceit and pleasure beyond
your wildest dream.

But …..is that enough for you to forget that girl?

Remember…..she dreamt about that prince charming that would treat
her like a princess.

Why do you continue to act out of desperation?

You were ok that hot August day you entered that Nissan stanza

Why did you fall in love heart?

The things I despised most about my childhood are now my reality.

Now I understand my mother's pain!

Is it better to be lonely than in love with someone who's in love with another?

But why does my body yearn for him so much?

Why does my heart rip apart when he goes through that door?

I MUST fix this stupid head, heart and body!

FREE FALL

I sometimes forget that I am worthy

Life's burdens are heavy

My crazy brain refuses to rest

My heart is ready to protest

Then I get a glimpse of you

I've been ensnared by lies

Experienced darkness in the light

Longed for a sacred dance with life

Or an embrace to warm my thighs

You untangled my feet

I've had torrential rains

The earth beneath me soaked away

Just as I'm about to fall

Your love surrounds me

And I feel safe

You are the match that lit my wick

The stream channeling my pathway to the sea

The wind strumming my strings

Although I hover above the clouds

But I'm free falling

In my resolute stance to resolve my pain, my heart whipped up another plan. There were no scripts to read, just me and my pain. I searched for a familiar place. One that will reduce the turmoil within. I couldn't calm my galloping heart or soothe my lost and afraid mind. I begged…..

BE MY ANCHOR

When the truest and best in me is all but tattered and torn

And my heart sings the melody of the dejected and forlorn

When there is no end to the raging sea that I am sailing on

I bid you, be my anchor in the midst of the gathering storm

When the cruel weight of unreal expectations gathers to wear me down

And my heart's light is dimmed by my penchant frown

When the raging tempest of this life toss me around

I bid you, be the mizzenmast that keeps me steadily sailing on

When I wrestle with this frail body and gets trampled by my own two
feet

And I am forced to see myself as a broken house of muscle bones and
meat

That forgets the grandeur of my strength so grand deeds cannot repeat

I bid you be the hull of the vessel that keeps me sailing troubled waters
deep

When my belief in me has waned enough so self-doubts are enhanced

And the curvature of my spine and knees become more pronounced and
advanced

When I can no longer see your face on which with favour I had glanced

I bid you, be the yards that bears the sails that keeps my floating soul
balanced

When the darkness gathers and finally steals the light

And the fleeting wings of my youth has been set to flight

And I am beset by demons from all sides in a fierce and brutal fight

I bid you, be as the mighty ship of state that keeps me sailing in the
mystery of the night

LOVE ME

I wish you wouldn't fall for me

Because I'm recklessly brave

Or when my enthusiasm

Is nothing but an extravagant rave

Don't love me when my body is primped

Head to toes outlandishly distinct

And I become your fantasy

I don't want your love

If it doesn't reach for similar things

Or mend my broken wings

So together we can fly to highest heights

For when the scales fall from your eyes

You'll see there's no disguise

And your infatuation will cease to rise

But love me when my old and wrinkled face

Is stone cold and emote

Or its color is far gone

Because I've forgotten who I am

Love me through my mess

Though it may be heightened stress

Then I will know that you love me

CAGED

There is a closet filled with clothes I cannot wear

Fine Jewelry kissing velvet but with my arms will never share

My blistered feet and broken knees now needs repair

And I stress about the job that gives me great fear

I long for the one who will embrace me like the spring morning air

Someone who brings back the sparkle of my jaded eyes as they stare

And whisper life into my waiting ears

But if only there was such one there would be no despair

This mysterious silence has made my heart cold

For the loneliness of nights tramples my soul

But this fairytale planted in my brain still remains untold

It awaits my knight in armor to reveal the secrets of old

The finger that writes our names in the sky

Tell of immense joy in a flash of its naked light

It releases our caged hearts so they will fly

High above the boundaries of human life

When that beautiful voice bellows my name

And from my heart lose all the bonding chains

I will fly into the sunset and the pouring rain

To reclaim my place in this fool's game

Moments

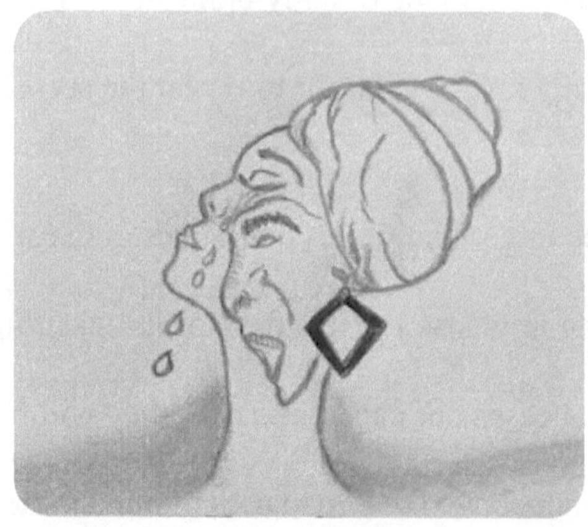

These are the moments

When lonely voices speak in my head

Giving their overwhelmingly sad comments

To a wayward mind in a lonely bed

They held hostage my will

When in the arms of darkness, I lay still

A wounded soldier with cries so shrill

And towering captors that boast their battle kill

They tell me of my failures and discontentment

And all the things others thought but never said

Though this adversary be the mother of torments

It's an enemy who became my best friend

With a loosely knitted basket I carry my fears

And a promise to save me from drowning in this sea of tears

But in the distance the grim reaper draws near

Cause this torture I can no longer bear

If ever these moments reappear

I'll tell them of the love we once shared

Then the lonely voices that speak

Will at last be loving and meek

Heart bottom

The bottom of my heart is a desolate place

Yet it is the place from which I create

There lie sediments of all I am

It is the place from which I soar

Still the place that kills my flight

The bottom of my heart is a place that does not sleep

It stirs my world violently sometimes making me weep

Normal boundaries for it does not exist

But it's humanness will always persist

The seat of my experience lies deep in that place

If beauty and glory could stimulate

It's joys, laughter, peace, and eradicate all hate

Then this crippled life will begin to recreate

The bottom of my heart is a pick me upper

A bedrock

A rock bottom

A sunlit morning

The dark cloud before the raindrops

The dew just before dawn

The peak I long to reach

The midnight

It's grateful

Rags to riches

Valley's mountains

Complete

But with others it won't ever compete

The bottom of my heart is an enchanted place

It belongs to the light

The dark

The angels

The demons

It's a tower of strength

A frail wooden bench

It's summer and fall

One that keeps me warm when winter calls

Known by a million names

Selfless but seeks no fame

Welcome to the bottom of my heart!

THE DREAM

I dreamt of the deceit and the pain

That's now messing with my brain

I saw the never ending dancing in the rain

And the rendezvous on Nigerian planes

As I listened to her claim to your name

It fueled immeasurable disdain

Not for the women who live on your lane

Or for the one who played me like a game

But the life I lived in vain

And myself who I now blame

I dreamt that I walked away

Not because I didn't want to stay

But I had to find a way

To keep the regretful tears at bay

For my love with pain, you repay

And my heart by a black knight did slay

If I could wipe away the memories stuck on replay

Or lessen the shock and dismay

Then I could continue to dream about that perfect day

When in your arms I'll be to stay

I dreamt of the melodies the hearts sing

The day you slipped on her wedding ring

The ones of soul ties with heavenly strings

And all those Mr and Mrs things

For when from a pillow she removed your ring

And slipped it over your velvet skin

There was celebration among your kin

To welcome the happiness it will bring

For they thought it was your greatest win

But my heart forever lost its rhythm

I dreamt I heard Congo drums deep in my ear

And saw African hips locked in patterns that's rare

I smelled the food scents travel through the atmosphere

And taste the love that both of you share

But if for a moment I could interfere

To snatch you from this matrimonial affair

I'd take you far into the stratosphere

With only you and me living there

But wishes are not horses to ride anywhere

So in shock I sit and stare

I dreamt you looked into her eyes

And said the words I now despise

I dos have become the greatest lies

Cause it binds unworthy lives

How can I loosen the soul ties

To undo all these terrible lies

For I am spiraling to my demise

If I could just awaken to realize

That by my side you'll always reside

Then my dream will never materialize

DROWNING...

I bring myself to the water's edge

For its tranquil sounds to soften my roaring head

It whispered soothingly in my ears

The price I'm paying isn't worth a drop of my tears

I peeped past the clear blue surface

And saw someone staring back at me

There was no fire in her eyes

Like I had when I looked at mine

I tried to bring myself to swim

But my strength forgot to check in

My opened mouth refused to scream

When being drowned by this tranquil stream

The struggle became all too real

I took another look and then had to choose

Between the drowning version of myself

And the one who will live to love again

In this river I left my fears

Watched its copious flow steal my tears

Taking them farther than I could've gone

To finally restore my peaceful child

I HAD TO LEAVE

I had to leave because I lost myself

I searched for the part of me that you would accept

Ignoring all of me

And now it's time

Time to breathe

Time to smile

Time to look deep in my soul

And find me

We all have decisions to make

Good or bad depends on your take

In this I thought you had a stake

But since you don't

I'm ready to leave this sleep and awake

To the harsh reality of losing me

And I'm disappointed

So I had to leave

It's going to be a roller coaster ride

Only because I pour out all of me from inside

Even that I tried to deny

Picking up the pieces is never easy

So I give myself grace

Grace to admit my faults

Grace to endure through it all

Grace to regain my peace and heal

Only then will I find me!

Letting go is never easy. Especially when time has grown on you. After 10 years, several things have now become a habit. You almost begin to feel entitled. But there comes a time that one must define what letting go means. People grow at different paces. Physical and mental maturity doesn't equate to emotional maturity. It doesn't mean that when people are apart, they must stop loving each other. In fact, the opposite is true. We learned that relationships that "work" must include cohabitation - and that one man should commit to one partner. And to some extent, I agree (especially when children are involved). However, not everyone was meant to follow that path. The pain of letting go is like a drug addict being weaned off an addictive substance. The dependency has to break and like a newborn being introduced to life outside of the womb, the work has just begun.

LETTING GO

I didn't let you go because I stopped loving you

In fact I let go because I was too in love

I couldn't allow us to damage US

Because what we have is greater than us

So I had to let go to preserve a perfect love

I didn't let go just yesterday

It's been a while since your blind actions

Triggered calculated reactions

And my tears followed a stream

To an ocean of dreams

I didn't find you there

I didn't let go of us

I let go of you

The distracted you

The one whose touch became a chore

No longer in sync with what's required to restore

Unconsciously stepping back

Failing to recognize the stack

Of signals that I'm letting go

I started letting go when we argue about how I feel

Repeating the same things I said

But you didn't realize because you've stopped listening

I wasn't enough for you and it didn't feel like home

I let go to give you space

I couldn't stand missing you while we're in the same place

DESTINY

Now that we meet at last

When will our hands clasp

Neither of us could pass

This magnetic field between our space

Oh universe……why did you allow this

Like the sun and the moon

Our time didn't come too soon

Though we briefly met one Sunday afternoon

Drifting along separately through our gloom

Were we meant to create this dune

Oh universe…is this the route to our doom

Destiny smiled our way one day

Determined to bind our hearts today

Forces threaten to push us far astray

Why bring us together if we're not meant to stay

I know strong love will keep them at bay

Oh universe…..This inexplicable madness is driving me insane

FINAL MOMENTS

Days of dread and fear are here

Peeps through the fog and draws my tears

An uncontrolled ocean suddenly appears

From the flood that my heart couldn't bear

My muffled voice tries to screams aloud

I cannot explain how fast my heart pounds

Unfathomable disbelief is all I've found

Goodbyes can't merely fit into words

The pictured scenes replay in my head

The life we had was woven well

From bits and pieces to whistles and bells

Reduced to a short summary that abruptly end

These final moments are a fiery hell

I pray to God this fury to quell

Take my soul and make it whole

Remove the thorns replace it with a rose

Is it the End?

It has come to the end

No more time together we'll spend

Since we're not going to make amends

My heart will miss your world without end

I would have followed you into the night

Cause equal and opposite spirits shouldn't fight

You were the one that matched even my might

And kept me calm when I find myself in a plight

My warrior spirit is now broken

My gut wrenched at the words spoken

Hammered my pride into the ground

I search for the me that can't be found

I had a haunting loneliness in my soul

Anxiety ever pressing upon my mole

Dancing with a heart that's cold

I had to leave so it wouldn't take a toll

In our quest for the perfect us

Our souls failed to shake the dust

Ignoring the beauty within

Cloudy hearts can never win

You were not a perfect man

But for me a most perfect one

Even the incredibly beautiful sea

Has infinite darkness we'll never see

In my heart you remain special

Though distance seems impossible to bridge

I can say I've found the only one

Who was made for my hand

There will be good days, then the bad days. Some days I want to reverse my decision, some days I am resolute. Every place is a reminder of the great times we had. But the bad time kept stealing.

SOMETIMES

What if I couldn't see the path I walked

Or touched the hand that led me across

If my breath wouldn't surrender to your embrace

Wrapped in a sea of pain you refuse to erase

Then I would be free to explore the depths of me

But sometimes….

If I could just get one peak of your face

It would bring out the light in my day

And give me vigor to sustain this pace

So when the baton is passed in this race

I'll sprint beyond the finish gate

But sometimes….

The days are often long and cold

My body aches from growing old

This seething furnace is reduced to coal

And my senses miss the smell of your cologne

That use to propel me leaps and bounds

But sometimes….

The best of me I'm yet to see

Cause it's wrapped up inside of us

If the incandescent vitality locked in this box

Could escape these drowning dark seas

A colorful masterpiece it will release

But sometimes….

As my days fade into eternal nights

And I lose the strength to fight

I pray for a glimmer of delight

To get me through these difficult times

So I can dream

But sometimes….

LONELY SOUL

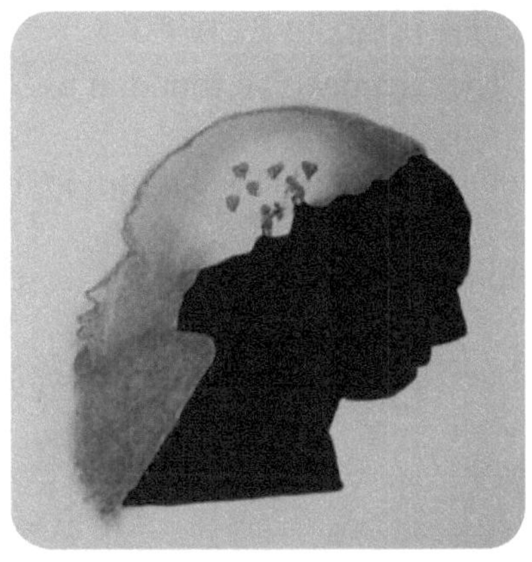

There's a haunting loneliness deep in my soul

One that filters the joy that makes me whole

Digs a deep well that drowns future goals

Down memory lane ain't a great place to stroll

Your heart was the place I called home

Sheltered me from the fears I bemoan

Strummed my strings stirred a sweet groan I beg

Til the day you left me here all alone

Oh love why must childhood folly punish future years

Come rest your cares upon my breast

Remake my house into a perfect home

Rekindle the fire that now refuse to burn

The friend we've found in us

That binds strong till we return to dust

Holds memories and builds trust

Even when after others we lust

When alone in our distant space

And I cannot feel or taste

The one I long to embrace

I'll be lonely for a while just in case

The night goes on at a slow pace

REWIND

If I could go back in time

I'd snatch the smallest moments

Sporadic unintentional and divine

That left the biggest imprint deep inside

Opportunities often missed

And words though slow to give

Sometimes are better left unsaid

For the sake of emotions you'll relive

The scratches and bruises of life

Etches in the heart a bleeding wound

Time and space will fail to erase

But will teach a lesson about grace

If I could rewind

The moments I shared with you

I'd strum those endless intimate strings

Of tunes that only we could sing

RUN

I want to be like the sun in the eastern sky

Peep through the clouds as the days go by

Climb the incline of the mountains high

And rest at midday while ordinary folk's toil

I want to be like the moon and stars

Lighting dark paths across space and time

Casting light shadows to brighten lover's shine

Awakening once dormant mystery rhymes

I want to run like the panther's chase

Into the fiery storm of your embrace

Leave all troubles accompanying this race

Let me run to you

Distance Reign

When sailing blindly down separate seas

That flows through life's oceans depth

I plead for your calm waters against my waves

Your opposing winds to balance my sails

The distance between the path I'll pass

Tortures my hull that seats my masts

Threatening the strength I need to cross

Lend me an outstretched hand with a loving clasp

Who then will God send to rescue me

With Aaron's hand in this distant land

To part this great unforgiving sea

Or dock my majestic ship on pure white sand

Til the hum of this sacred dream

Breathes life into my veins

I'll continue this treacherous sail

Hoping distance will break its cruel reign

IRREVERSIBLY

This broken record attempts to play

The craziest songs on the gloomiest days

Scratching and sticking at the happy lines

I wish I could go back in time

If my weathered heart could make a wish

It would be to rewind the lines I missed

The ones that felt like I was being kissed

The sweetest taste from those honey lips

But now it's wrinkled and old

With memories that's precious like fine gold

When this body is finally cold

This irreversible love will warm my soul

HOME

On separate journeys we will tread

Trekking across plains and seas

Some valleys will seem like mountains

But you'll always be home for me

My heart was filled with ardent care

For someone I wish would hold me dear

Under one sky my spirit danced with yours

Wondering when cupids arrow would hit my core

A desolate life this if surrounded by just people

Or dim stars that line the midnight skies

For when the heart stares dead in beauty's eyes

A perfect match it will recognize

How distant can twin hearts be

When not defined by the length of the sea

Though physicality is like oblivion's spring

But you'll always be home for me

There is so much beauty to be found in LOVE, yet so much PAIN. I've learned that love is best when it is allowed room to grow. When held too tightly, it will vanish into thin air or prevailing circumstances will allow it to die a natural death. It doesn't matter what the circumstance, LOVE lingers still. The love that learns to let go of all attachments, results/outcomes, and preconceived ideas. I've had to unlearn the lessons I've learned about what a perfect love should be. My idea of the white picket fence, the children, the husband, and "the life" were accumulations of the fairytale that is only played out on TV. My disappointments, although real, may have been lessened had I learned to see love for what it is. Releasing the "conditions" may be painful, but it is necessary to grow in love. Operating in fear negates the common good that can be had from love. "There is no fear in love; but perfect love casteth out fear: because fear hath torment. He that feareth is not made perfect in love" (KJV 1 John 4:18). The passion, excitement, butterflies, hurt, pain, and gains are all used to measure love. They may be valid measurements, but when the dust settles, they are subjective measurements. Too often we fall into a trap and when our expectations are not met, we go into a downward spiral. Society's definition doesn't have to be mine. We all get to experience life as individuals and collectively. There is nothing wrong with going against the grain, unpopular as it may be. The experiences we attach to love may have no bearing on love. At birth, we were never given a script. We picked up all our learnings along our journey. What we chose to adapt is never anyone's fault. However, life will throw us some lessons that will either confirm or challenge our way of being. When two imperfect people decide to become one, there may be chaos. They not only accumulate ideas of what love should be, but they carry baggage from their individual lives. It may take a lifetime to resolve the baggage. They may never be able to totally understand each other. But love becomes a dance of meeting each other where they are at.

THE LANGUAGE OF LOVE

I'm learning to love you in a new way

One that will allow you to stay

Closer than the leaves and wind in a sway

Know that I won't ever get in your way

When the beautiful you go on display

I'm learning to love you more from a place

Where selfish intentions have no space

To tango or run like they're in a race

Fighting for your heart has no base

I don't own you so I'll appreciate this pace

I'm learning of a love that'll set us free

On eagle's wings together we'll fly atop trees

Experience breathtaking views only angels see

Massaging clouds to look like you and me

Wearing crowns meant for the king in you and queen in me

I'm learning a love that teaches all I don't know

One that gives us free will so we can grow

In unison of hearts that will always flow

Creating an "US" that will make minds blow

Then We'll float around like angels with a glow

I'm learning to love you even if you leave

This special love will mend and heal hearts that grieve

No more tight holds I will let you breath

Build you strong so you'll never bleed

I am learning to love you!

Deep and Dark Place

He said he loved me

That I'm the ONLY one who stirs his pot

Though it may be filled with well-rehearsed plots

And repeated scenes of applause less acts

That serves to fuel his fears and diminish his cares

But he said he loved me

From a deep and dark place

I scream aloud the whispers of love

Hoping they'll shower down blessings from above

And bring forth gentleness like a dove

Or a dim light to soften the darkness

So his eyes can be relit

But he said he loved me

From a deep and dark place

There's a man that hides in that dismal place

Possessing all the secrets of the survivor's game

A warrior against himself and everyone who came

Living through self-fulfilling prophecies

That drives a wedge between him and himself

But he said he loved me

From a deep and dark place

Along the spectacular landscapes of his mind

Lives a little boy inside

Scared of the place where he resides

Buried deep beneath the rubble of disguise

The noise within silent but deafening

Still he said he loved me

From a deep and dark place

I pray for an escape

The view from here is not so great

If I could reach him beyond that spot

That blinds the panoramic view of all he's got

Notwithstanding this fight and his loss

Still he loved me

From a deep and dark place

So I honor that place

Though I may never experience it's embrace

Or walk along the therapeutic path it creates

But for him it must be a beautifully frightening space

Cause if that's where his heart and soul resides

I'll love him back

From my deep and dark place

I Never Left

You and I will be inseparable till death

Even though physically we couldn't nest

This unbreakable bond defies even the fiercest attack

I'm on the edge of the bluest seas radiating dreams cause I never left

The flow of the tide may break our sails

Life's winds may gust but we're not frail

Shallow heights may seem impossible to scale

But we won't lose sight of the sweet gale that warms our breast

When our final waltz we'll take

And the open grave awaits

Our hearts will occupy that sacred space

That our infinite journey will create

AWAKEN

I soared across the open skies

Over great firmaments and celestial tides

Trying to find some happy times

If there was just someone by my side

And when I settled on the one I knew

Because he said he'll never be untrue

But his mind concocted another brew

That controlled his entire attitude

For all the reasons I became distraught

And all the deceptions that I fought

Through the gates of hell I eventually walked

To learn the lessons that it taught

So I went on a journey on the inside

For what I couldn't see with these frail eyes

And then I finally realized

That my happiness was within me the whole time

Now I can see myself as a prize

And appreciate experiences with which I reside

I thank the one who chose to wear a disguise

For it awakened my sleeping eyes

Life after heartbreak will never be the same. The treacherous journey to healing included getting to know "ME." And having to sit with me was no joke. Deciding to heal from his mistakes meant also looking at mine, at least if I were to be honest with myself. It is no longer a blame game. But the work must be done. Conquering self is essential to pure love. My grandfather once told me that every problem has a solution and time will answer every question. I could hear him in my head guiding me on days when I don't want to be bothered. I had a friend that I could share my most intimate thoughts with and be confident that she would honor my feelings. Sher was my sounding piece, and I burdened her ears. There were times when I would not say anything for fear of her getting tired of me. So, I confided in my notepad. I found my talents through heartbreak.

Thinking Woman

Oh gates of hell how you dance for me

And make my eyes overflow with bitter tears

And lay bare my heavy anxiety exposing my fears

Unfathomable pain leaving nothing to gain

The abyss of time lost in your immeasurable space

My heavy head upon a right hand of fate

And a left Knee bears the brunt of gravity

What's on your mind? You may ask

Am I afraid to tame the horses in my head

Or has my conceit deluded me into believing there's peace of mind

Ponderous burdens on the back I wear

I'm Trying to decipher here I swear

But when it rains it pours my dear

Is it like this with you? Are you constantly in despair too?

Does your world flash in front of you or is what I feel very rare?

Why does mine refuse to rest or clear?

When all I want to do is repair

The things I may have done to cause you to stare

And in your mind I may be mentally unprepared

Oh gates of hell why do you call?

I know your fury on me you wish would fall

You would devour me and leave my loved ones to bawl

Cripple my limbs like a pit bull you would maul

Making it seem like you and I are in a brawl

But I'm a thinking woman with skills that are deflectable and raw.

BROKEN PIECES

Extraordinary beauty lies

Where broken pieces reside

Growing anew from the earth

Evolving through various stages from birth

Torn apart then built up

In broken pieces lies the good stuff

It's incandescent masterpiece

Appeared full and complete

Perfect in every way

But as such was never meant to stay

The cracks of circumstances and vile attacks

Refines it aglow with ardor that's exact

The whispers round about it hear

Sprinkles lightly spotted dust to smear

Slowly covering its glow

Until energy forgets to flow

The morning will usher anew

Til bursts of light begins to shine through

Embrace the broken pieces of you

For these are the parts that carry you through

The trauma that you refuse to face

Is the treadmill to speed up your pace

Give it a voice so it can speak

Then sit back and watch it peak

Boldness will awaken in her eyes

Resonate even with those who despise

Occurring repeatedly strengthening her strides

Killing the putrid stench of bloodlines

Emerging rejuvenated from the ash

Newness of beauty shining like cash

I RISE

I rise with my fears

Wash them away with tears

Reach deep in my gut

When I feel I ain't got enough

If ever I appear

That there's a weak gear

Don't be fooled

I'll still run my race like a mere

I rise with love

Ready to sprinkle all about

For therein lies a well

That's bigger than I can tell

I will freely give

And I am not naive

But a heart made of gold

Can never grow old

I rise today empowered

I am all I need

To accomplish with great speed

The task I must complete

I know there's a hand

Outstretched to help me stand

I thank you my dear

Now I won't rise with any fears

THE PAINTER'S PIECE

If I were a prolific painter

With non other to compare

My best work would tell the enchanted story

Of two lover's secret tale

Or draw the missing strokes

To be the perfect fairy tale

Their star light beamed from the distant sky

It's axis originating way up high

A triangular path to be made a straight line

And bodies to be intertwined

So at the perfect time

Fate would have it all aligned

In one stroke of luck, I dipped my brush

Traced his journey to her in a colorful rush

For it was time for their hands to touch

And be their summer's day August crush

His chariot seats were not as plush

But his invite was good enough

Colors like fireworks canopied the skies

The angels in heaven sang hallelujahs on high

The firmament bowed to kiss the earth's cries

And butterflies fluttered by their sides

In solemn celebration and heart stopping delight

As they gazed into each other's eyes

The colors then began to fade

When reality returned to their gaze

For his heart was wrapped in jade

While hers was youthful and craved an escapade

But their fire always stayed

Like an Olympic Torch throughout the pouring rain

As I dipped my brush in the pool of luck

To brighten up the paths that seemed too rough

I recalled that the rough stuff

May break some bones or cause some cuts

But they heal with skin that's tough

So I gently laid down my brush

Then I let the magic brush glide

Filling the canvas with whatever it decides

Even heartbreaking deceptive lies

There were flowers along the paths

And oceans that they must cross

But their hearts remained as one even when they didn't understand

The greatest painters that will ever live

Who possess the most beautiful artistic skills

Will retell this story of love in exceptional ways

Or create a sequel for their own sake

But rivals they will never be

For this painter's piece remains unique

WARRIOR'S RACE

Her illuminating grace and strength

Outlives the eastern sun

The shadow that is cast

Is one that will forever last

Amidst her effervescent light

A dance of love and great might

A concoction that only few

Can admit they ever knew

On the quest for success

With ambition and a powerful mindset

Focused on passing the tests

And ignoring all the rest

Strapping on the breastplate of courage

Persevering through brokenness

Walking barefooted through the valley of the shadow of death

And fearing no obstacles to beset

When up against the battlefield

Her prayer filled weapon she'll wield

Calls on her army's angel squad

Whose power and presence is iron clad

Head tilted backward in upright stance

Proudly wearing her crown of circumstance

Folding powerful hands across her chest

Confident that she's done her best

Beneath the beauty of warm smiles

Lies a soul that's rear and fierce

Dressed in bravery's margaric gown

Running her race without a frown

The torch she carries now

She'll pass on then take a bow

When at the end of her unparalleled pace

A warrior's race she'll end with grace

20 years had passed. It still felt like yesterday. My head wanted one last moment….at least so I thought. Unresolved passion and distance tugged at me. I couldn't resist.

HEART'S EYES

The years crept across my once silk skin

Inviting gravity to move on in

Honey golden

Use to be chocolate brown tint

Reduced to freckle tainted quilts

My youthful glow eluded my grasp

Flashes of beauty gives a distant wink

In the mirror stands my mortal enemy still

I don't recognize her

Yet they say its image is perfect

I long to see that smile on his face

Those stares that pierced deep into my soul

Unquenched fire penetrating my skin

Emotionally and intellectually akin

Is it just me or he misses these too

I hear his breath in between sobs

Warmth still pressed against my thighs

One of a kind embrace chase away the day

As he puts my fears to rest

Whispers the sweetest thing I've ever heard

I only see you through my heart's eyes

Revolutionary Love

You won't stay angry

For anger breeds contempt

Or willful disregard for one part of you

Leaving your Siamese heart with a feeling of dismemberment

Love is cruel like a wizard's spell

For it keeps all its secrets well

When it is good it's all whistles and bells

But when broken it will plunge you straight to hell

It causes you to tend to your grief

Fully aware the effects are not brief

Powerful tremors shake apart twin hearts

Then bleeding arteries soak through your chest

Bad memories continuously haunt

Like a snake they slither up your limbs

You must fight like an eagle In thin air

Raise the bar until their potency disappear

You'll long to find relief

For your weeping eyes must heal

This gaping hole in your soul

Swallows your heart and makes you cold

You'll be ready to forgive

Even though you won't ever forget

A revolutionary love like ours

Is much too valuable to regret

Best Friends

My greatest friends were never my foes

For they guide me to where I must go

If ever there are things that I should know

I call on the ones that help me grow

Sadness and sorrow can be a thunderous storm

But it only serves to make me calm

Reminding me that alone I will never survive

It is deep connections that keep me alive

The anger that I chose to suppress

Prevents me from getting myself into a hot mess

For when it dies a natural death

No consequences are left to address

Fear and anxiety are identical twins

Which sometimes seek to clip my wings

It alerts me to possible dangerous things

That may jeopardize my ability to win

Guilt and shame sometimes play a shrewd game

Questioning my humanness and laying down blame

But if I'm checked by these proficient whips

Then the lessons life throw at me will forever stick

Confusion is my cue to seek clarity

Stimulating my brain to question such disparity

I'm black you're not but I won't accept your negativity

Let's plan to share this vast prosperity

Regret is my truest distant friend

It seldom visits and we never contend

For on the treacherous path ahead

All my best friends endure to the very end

Hushed

When my motion is hushed and I'm paralyzed

Melodic rhythms of the orchestra will find its way

For I've danced a million waltz under moonlit skies

And only you complete the symphonic picture of light

When my heartbeat is hushed in this mortal being

It will not cease to roar like an African drum

A tune that only you could strum

Soothed by the upward sweep of your thumb

When my voice is hushed by that final silence

I hope you know that I've given my all

Those midnight serenades you never heard

Warms my breast when my soul is at rest

When tomorrow is hushed by time

And tears cannot reclaim mine

I wish you wouldn't cry as you did yesterday

Cause my love will remain with you always

When my dreams are hushed by a wand

An angel came and took me by the hand

Gave me wings so I could stand

I'll fly away to wait for you beyond this land

www.ingramcontent.com/pod-product-compliance
Lightning Source LLC
Chambersburg PA
CBHW061438210726
48287CB00007B/2259